Key Weird

Robert Tacoma

Mango Press
Gainesville, Florida

For information address
Mango Press
P.O. Box 141261
Gainesville, FL 32614-1261
mangopress@gmail.com

This is a work of fiction. Names, characters, places, and
incidents either are products of the author's imagination or
are used fictitiously. Any resemblance to actual events or
locales or persons, living or dead, is entirely coincidental.

For information on books by Robert Tacoma:
www.tacobob.com
mangopress@gmail.com

Front cover illustration by Greg Hatcher.
Back cover illustration by Greg Hatcher and Xiola.
Book cover and interior design by Merrey Design.

First U.S. edition published 2005.
Printed in the United States of America by Morris Publishing.

ISBN: 0-9760630-0-X

10 9 8 7 6 5 4 3 2 1

For my father
for all those wonderful trips to the Keys
when I was a kid

When the going gets weird,
the weird turn pro.

— H.S. Thompson

Key Weird

Chapter 1

Lone Star Ranching for Taco Bob

"Hard work and easy rocking."

My ranch wasn't always a lake. In fact, at one time it had been one of your more prosperous possum ranches in the Armadillo, Texas, area. But due to a run of mighty poor luck involving Mother Nature and the government, I was down to my last few dollars, the name Taco Bob, and a soggy ranch house. With the way current events had been stacking up, I decided my best course of action would be to sit out on the front porch and have a short one while I tried to make sense of it all.

I got settled good in my rocking chair and picked up my afternoon crossword puzzle. I needed a seven letter word for bad news that started with an "s." I was giving that some thought when I noticed a county police car coming down the highway about a mile away.

I tried a sip of whiskey and took a quick count of the fingers on my left hand. During a recent stay at the county jail,

1

I'd read this book called *Dreaming for the Easily Led*. The fella writing the book said you had to count your fingers a lot if you wanted to enter into the exciting and mysterious world of Lucid Dreams. Always willing to try something new, and not having much else to do at the time, I'd gotten into the habit of seeing how many fingers I had.

When I looked up from my latest digit reconnaissance, it looked like the Sheriff himself taking the turn that would bring him down what was left of my driveway. I wrote the word down in the crossword.

*   *   *

My life has had its ups and downs, and up until a few weeks earlier I'd been enjoying the ride on one of the better ups for several years. A lot of hard work and a good dose of luck had me sitting on a nice ranch of prime possum pasture just as the blackened-possum craze was sweeping the country. It was a tough job keeping up with the little nocturnal marsupials, but the financial rewards made it worthwhile.

In fact, things were going so well there for a while, I'd remodeled the big house, built a bunkhouse for the boys working on the ranch, and ever the entrepreneur, even gotten into raising gators on the side.

Just when it was looking like I had life by the tail, things started slipping away. It was small things at first. Like the locusts and late freeze wiping out most of the cornfields and vegetable gardens. Stuff like that.

Then along came the tornado. Lost the big barn with most of the possums and my new bass boat that night. Tore up the house pretty good too. A few days later we'd just about got the roof fixed on the house, and what possums were left squared away, when the prairie fire came through. So that kept us busy.

Lost the bunkhouse and the rest of the crops and what livestock was left that day. Probably would have lost the house in the fire as well if it hadn't started raining. It was a good rain too. So good it kept raining all that night and the next day and busted the levee and flooded the whole area, mostly my ranch.

Then the help all quit. Can't blame 'em much though, hard to be a possum rancher when all the possums are gone and the ranch is under several feet of water.

At that point I didn't see how things could get much worse.

That's when the first of the metal drums came to the surface of the lake that looked like it had settled in for good over my ranch. The water started getting a yellow tinge to it, and was not smelling all that great either. Before long there were lots of drums floating around, and the government sent some fellas in helicopters wearing those white spaceman suits to check 'em out. Turns out, they were drums of toxic waste that'd been buried out there before I bought the place. The very same place I had got such a good deal on buying from the government.

Then the sheriff showed up one day and said he had to put me in jail for running a toxic waste dump without a permit. I asked him how I was supposed to get one of these permits, and he said they stopped giving those out years ago. So it was off to jail and some light reading for me.

Old Man Jennings in town got a son that forsook taking over the family moonshine business and run off to the big city to lawyer school. I got a hold of him, and after a few days and most of the rest of my money, he convinced the government I wasn't the one been burying drums of toxic waste on the ranch several years before I bought it. So I was once again a free man, though severely financially challenged.

* * *

When the help all left, Hop Chong, the ranch cook, doctor, and bookkeeper, decided to stick it out a while longer. The little Chinaman came out of the house and stood there next to me as that big ol' sheriff waded over from where he'd parked his car. I remained reclining in my rocker, steadfastly holding onto my drink, my crossword, and the knowledge that the sheriff ain't ever come around with anything approaching good news. Hop was almost as stubborn as me, and said he was sticking it out 'til the bitter end, which looked like it had just walked up the front porch steps.

"Morning, Taco Bob."

"Morning, Sheriff."

He gave my sole remaining employee, and good friend, a hard look and a nod. "Hop."

The little man always had him a case of the deep-seated resentment toward any kind of law enforcement personnel. I'd never asked, but I think it had something to do with a place called Tiananmen Square over there in China.

Though he'd learned to speak a passable form of Texas English, Hop let loose with a long, fast, run of Chinese that sounded to me like it contained detailed comparisons of the sheriff and canine intestinal miseries.

The sheriff started fingering the snap on his holstered firearm, and Hop's hand was easing down into his apron, where he was known to keep a rather formidable butcher knife. I lit up my best smile.

"So what brings you out to my humble abode on this beautiful day, Sheriff?" Just as I said that, there was a rumble of thunder and it started raining. The sheriff broke off the stare-down going on between him and Hop. The Man cleared his throat a good one and gave his squeaky leather cop belt a quick adjustment.

"Taco Bob, by the power vested in me by the great state of Texas, I'm here to inform you that your ranch has been condemned and pronounced unsafe for human occupation. This here means y'all gotta git!"

Due to the recent rapid spiral of events down life's toilet, this didn't surprise me much. The bright side being I didn't see how anything could be much worse.

Hop, however, who was still giving the sheriff the evil eye, took the news a little hard and commenced to growling. He started showing some yellow teeth through the snarl, and had his hand all the way down in his apron. The Sheriff kept talking while backing down the steps.

"Y'all got 'til tomorrow morning to vacate these here premises." He slogged on back toward his cop car in the rain, then stopped. "I almost forgot to tell you. The Dalton Gang broke out of prison this morning!"

That was the thing that could be worse.

* * *

The next morning, Hop had his stuff all packed in the same big suitcase he had when I first laid eyes on him sitting there on the porch all them years earlier. I give him a ride into town where he was going to be staying with some kin and we said our goodbyes like real men, then got all teary-eyed and hugged big.

Which left me with a pickup truck, some camping and fishing stuff, a few clothes, and the rest of my life. I decided to leave town for a while, since things hadn't been going all that swell in the recent past and the immediate future seemed likely to involve a visit from the Daltons. I was thinking Florida; figured I might at least have a little better luck with the weather down there.

Chapter 2
That Old Black Magic

Years earlier, at the same time Taco Bob had first seen a Chinese gentleman named Hop Chong sitting on his front porch, a young woman in northern California sat down on a rock. It was a dreary day, and it looked like it might start raining again any minute.

The young woman, whose name at the time was Tula, didn't remember how long she'd been sitting on the rock. She might have blacked out for a minute or two. Normally, she didn't sit on rocks, especially wet, dirty rocks, but she was drunk enough she'd had to sit somewhere, right then.

Her party buddies were still in the tavern, way over there across the parking lot. A neon sign glared at her from above the door — The Busted Gut. Tula vaguely remembered coming outside to get some air; all the smoke in the bar was making her sick. Or it could have something to do with the coke she'd snorted, or the fact they'd been bar hopping for ten hours.

Something smelled rotten. The rock, not her. She smelled sweet — and it was the heavy sweetness of Calvin Klein mixing with the rock smell that made her stomach quake. Fighting back nausea, she got unsteadily to her feet. She had to go home. Now. Where was her ride, the red Cougar Devon what's-his-face had driven?

She staggered back to the tavern to find Devon and tell him to take her home NOW.

With wet rock crud smeared on the ass of her designer jeans, she navigated the dark, smoky bar with as much dignity as she could. She found her friends sitting at a table in the corner, laughing and pointing at her.

Screw 'em; who were they? Cindy always looked like she'd caught her hair in a fan, Devon had the fashion sense of a primate, and Lane was hung like a mouse.

She stood unsteadily before the table of giggling people, and with all eyes upon her, she said, "I want to go ho—" and barfed all over the table and everyone sitting at it.

*   *   *

The next afternoon, after coffee, orange juice, and another nap, she picked up the book her roommate Jenny was always talking about and started to read. This was the book that changed her life. Sorcery. Magical powers, mysterious spirits, all that. She could do this — well, she could learn to do it. At least some of it. Maybe if she got good enough, she wouldn't have to be nice to people anymore or work an actual job. Not to mention, anyone into that kind of stuff would need to wear all kinds of sexy sorceress clothes, and that was pretty cool too.

With the firm resolve that comes easily to the young and hungover, Tula swore she'd devote her life to the study of mysticism and the occult and never take drugs or drink again. Well, maybe not as much anyway, no sense in getting weird about it. She would read every book ever written on her new field of interest as well as fully investigate clothing options that would help her look and feel the part.

A few weeks later she had read through the good parts of at least three books on sorcery and the occult, and figured she had a handle on the stuff. She quit her job as cashier at the local Safeway and packed her new collection of mostly black lacy clothes, black nail polish, black lipstick, and assorted charms, crystals, and talismans. She made for Los Angeles in her aging Volkswagen to find some cool witches' covens, or sects, or something to hang out with.

Chapter 3

On the Road with Taco Bob

"Somewhere there's a fish with my name on it!"

It's a special kind of feeling when everything you own is in the back of a pickup truck, and you're heading down the road with no particular plans. I was trying hard to find the upside to my current situation and decided the only thing good about losing everything you worked so hard for is you pretty much lose the responsibilities too. So I felt like I was starting out with a clean slate as I left the Lone Star State, time to think about my next move in the great game of life.

After a few hours of driving and thinking, occasionally checking behind me for Daltons, I'd worked up a considerable thirst. Seeing billboards every few miles for a place on the Alabama–Florida border saying they had the coldest beer in the south might have had something to do with it. I decided to take on the responsibility of investigating such a wild claim myself, as a public service.

I finally found the place, and as advertised, it was right on the water, the very top of the Gulf of Mexico to be exact. A big place, looked kinda like a collection of well-worn road-houses and honky-tonks pushed together. I got the truck parked behind a convenient dumpster and ambled in.

It was right there on the state line all right. In fact, there was a big yellow dashed line running smack down the middle of the floor inside and across the bar. One side was done up with Alabama flags and a bunch of stuff about some bear football coach. The other side of the yellow line was plastic pink flamingos and palm trees. Both sides had the usual collection of stuff stuck on the walls and ceilings: autographed snapshots of people no one knew, old license plates, weird beer bottles, bumper stickers, and an assortment of ladies undergarments. I gawked on across the last few feet of Alabama and grabbed the first barstool in Florida. It was still early, but the place was already filling up. I got the attention of the cute gal behind the bar wearing a Florida Gators T-shirt.

"Afternoon, stranger. What'll ya have?"

"Afternoon. I'd be mighty proud to try one of those Coldest Beers in the South I been reading about the last hundred miles or so."

While she was attending to that, I did a little more gawking around. At a table nearby, some greasy, grubby types, who looked like they belonged to the shiny motorcycles parked neatly out front, were having a lively exchange on gas mileage and mullet throwing. In amongst the construction workers and fishermen was a sprinkling of tourists with the requisite cameras and sunburned knees. A couple of well-formed young women in bikinis came gliding through the bar with a well-practiced saunter. The biker's conversation took a sudden swing to female anatomy, starting with the chest area. My beer arrived.

"Here ya go, stranger."

"Thanks. What's all this going on over here?" I gestured toward the other side of the bar with one hand while directing a frosty mug toward my face with the other.

"Mullet throwing warm-ups. We got a big game coming up with New Orleans next week. Big rivalry, been going on for years."

She said something about a big stink last year involving a sandy mullet in a field goal situation, but the sensation of pouring cold beer down my road-parched throat had momentarily shut down all other sensory input. Then I noticed the big, tanned fella sitting next to me, on the Alabama side, looking my way, smiling.

"So is that the coldest beer, or what?"

"If it ain't, it's close enough for me." It took me a couple beats to get that out. The beer was so cold, it took my breath away.

"They got special computerized refrigeration going on, gets beer as cold as possible without actually freezing."

"You must be local then, knowing all that. Name's Taco Bob, I'm just passing through."

"Friends back home call me Roadkill Bill, Roadkill for short. Just passing by and stopped in for a quick one myself, barmaid filled me in on the beer thing." We reached over the state line and gave a good handshake. "This your first time in Florida?"

"Yep. Come here to try my hand at something different. Thought I'd give saltwater fishing a try, catch some of those marlins and sailfish and tarpon and such." I went on a bit more listing off some of the fish names I could remember from fishing shows, leading up to how I was hoping to come up on the Ultimate Fishing Experience. The more I went on, the better it sounded, at least to me. My new acquaintance didn't seem to share my enthusiasm.

"Well, I wish you luck on all that. I'm headed to Texas myself, hope to do a little ranching."

My attention wandered off, again. Three athletic and captivating young women started taking turns throwing a fish across the room into a barrel, and I was concentrating more on them than on the fella talking to me. Two of the women were the ones in the bikinis, the third was sporting a team jersey saying, "Sirens." I was spellbound. I even forgot about the crossword I had laid on the bar.

"… and that's when I decided to quit the fishing guide business in Florida and get into possum ranching out West." This brought me back. With a Herculean effort, I drug my eyes away from the three temptresses and looked over to see Roadkill paying his bill.

"Nice meeting you, Taco Bob. I gotta be getting down the road." And he was gone, leaving me with a mouthful of questions.

I wouldn't have minded another beer, nor would I have minded seeing the barmaid bending over that cooler digging out another frosty mug. But upon pondering my current financial situation, I determined it prudent to hit the trail again myself.

I was so much into being in Florida, I didn't want to go back to Alabama to get my truck. The three mesmerizing mullet throwers broke into an enchanting song about their team, but I walked across the state line and got to the door without stopping to listen.

I'm not normally a clumsy person, but for some reason I wasn't paying attention when I stepped outside, and stepped right on George Dalton's foot. It'd been a while since I'd seen the wiry little devil, so I might not have even realized it was him if it hadn't been for the big hunting knife he was pulling out of his belt with obvious intent.

Luckily, my reflexes took over long enough to give George a good kick in the knee as I spun back around for the front door. Blind fear being the great motivator it is, I was able to run through the bar and slip out the back door with a speed and agility that surprised many, including myself.

There appeared to be a marked increase in the noise level coming from inside the bar as I drove in a timely manner from the parking lot and on into Florida.

Chapter 4

Home Sweet Cult

The southern California cult scene. Strange people, stranger ideas. Tula fit right in and was learning fast.

"Hi, I'm Brad!"

"So, you worship sharks, is that the deal?"

After weeks of checking out cults she was up to S in the cult guide and still hadn't found what she was looking for.

"Sharks are so misunderstood! They respond to love just like we do!" The guy at the reception desk of Shark Luv Inc. was giving Tula a good looking-over and showing a lot of teeth, which she noticed were sharpened into points.

"What about sex? You're not having sex with sharks, are you?" She'd seen some strange shit lately and figured she might as well get to it.

"Heavens no! We just cuddle!" The guy pulled out a big stuffed shark from under the desk and started kissing it. She'd seen worse.

"No human sacrifices, torturing, or poison drinking?" Brad was really getting into it, dry humping the shark and trying to French kiss it. Yeah, that was pretty weird all right, but she'd seen weirder.

"We only love sharks! Nothing strange here!" The guy went to the carpet on top of the stuffed shark without breaking rhythm. "Moonfish will be here in a minute to show you around!"

Moonfish came in all smiles with typical glassy-eyed cult enthusiasm and the same pointed teeth. She stepped over Brad humping on the floor without a glance.

"Come with me and I'll show you the sacred shark-feeding tanks!" Moonfish kept smiling, gesturing toward the back door. She was missing an arm.

"Okay, sure. Let me just put something in my car first." And Tula headed out the door, put her ass in the car, and got the hell out of there.

* * *

"How'd the shark people go?" Tula's roommate was home.

"Not bad. I remembered I'm allergic to being eaten though, so I had to pass."

"Too bad. Hey, that really cool writer guy who wrote the book about dreaming is giving a talk at the bookstore this evening if you're interested."

"Maybe. You going?"

"Can't. Just started working on a new spell that's going to take all evening. Can I borrow your red candles and cloak?"

"Sure. So this guy is cool, huh?"

Her roomie, a supposedly reformed mall rat, was cooking up a potion in the kitchen. Beckoning the gatekeeper of shoe sales, probably.

"Way cool, and mysterious too! He's like a sorcerer or a shaman or something! I think he's also rich and lives in a big mansion."

This last bit caused one of Tula's eyebrows to raise.

"Oh, really?"

*   *   *

Bookstore smells. Squeaky plastic chairs. The man had charisma, grace, personality. The man had style.

After the talk, she waited until the groupie types that were shamelessly throwing themselves at the writer thinned out so she could have a serious and mature word with the man.

"I, uh, really love your books!"

Tula was wearing her best all-black outfit and trying hard to look mysterious. She looked hot, and knew it. The man's name was Charlie Spider, and he had a few years on her, quite a few, but his eyes smiled at her in a way that aroused more than just her curiosity.

"I can see your aura is strong; you are obviously a woman who knows what she wants. Perhaps you would like to come by later. I could show you something I'm working on for my next book, a technique called Dreaming Awake for the Sensuous Woman."

*   *   *

The mansion was huge, impressive, and a long way from pricing disposable diapers at the grocery store. When Tula walked through the doors of the grand old house, something happened inside her. It felt like she had come home.

*   *   *

Lotion, bath salts, glycerin soap, shower gel. All made with the best chocolate. She couldn't decide.

"I can't decide, they all look so good."

Charlie smiled his devilish smile.

"Why don't you try a little of each?"

Charlie was great, especially at first. He pampered and charmed. He filled her head with stories of magic and told her frequently how special she was, especially when she was in his bed.

"You remind me of the powerful Mexican sorceress in Oaxaca who wanted to turn me into a crow. She had a penchant for writers, that one, mystical writers in particular. Said she was doing the world a great service turning the worst of us into birds, then dispatching them to another dimension."

Charlie paused to light his medicine pipe. They shared a few puffs of the sweet smoke, but the storyteller seemed to have forgotten his story and was dreamily brushing her bare breasts with the back of his hand.

"So what happened? To the sorceress?"

Charlie looked up, surprised.

"I have no idea! When she turned me into a crow, I flew out of there as fast as I could and never went back!"

*　*　*

Charlie was a trip, all right. But as much as she was taken with the famous writer, she didn't really mind sharing him with the other women living there. Somehow, there always seemed to be enough of Charlie to go around.

Money didn't seem to be a problem, so that was cool. The only thing that sucked was he wanted all his girls to keep their hair short and dress rather plainly. So much for erotic fashions.

Charlie also had this thing about giving the women new names. He gave her a name that she would still have years later. They even went through the legal process to change her name to Carol. Carol Derrière.

Most of the other women at the mansion studied martial arts or sorcery, or took college courses. Though Carol liked to dabble in the odd occult practice from time to time, she devoted most of her time to pursuing the finer points of lounging and relaxing. And partying. God, but they had some great parties. It was an environment that allowed her to see others, especially those outside the Spider Cult, as the inferior beings she had always suspected they were.

Other than the clothes thing, Carol was quite content with her life as a pampered lady. She had found her calling. There didn't seem to be anything that could possibly go wrong.

Chapter 5

Panama City Welcomes Taco Bob

*"Only bad thing about smoking fish is
they're hard to keep lit."*

I decided to check out the Redneck Riviera. That's what
they call the panhandle area of Florida around Panama City.
Something to do with all those beautiful white sand beaches
just a beer-can throw away from Lower Alabama, known
locally as LA.

Panama City damn sure has some of the nicest beaches
I ever seen, all right, and the place was thick with Spring
Breakers. Some of the gals there at the beach were a sight
for a man who'd lived the last few years in a place where
the nearest woman was in a town miles away. Since I was
making all these fresh plans for the future, this put me in
mind to leave a little room in there somewhere in case I
should happen upon a lady who favored men with a promising future in trophy fish and a solid background in possums. You never know.

I came up on a little RV park not far from the beach where I could stay cheap. The widow-woman running the place offered to let me do some odd jobs to pay the rent and make a little pocket money. I liked the place right off, nice and quiet for crosswords and finger counting. There was swimming close by, friendly people, and that sea breeze coming in off the gulf. And no Daltons.

*   *   *

Several days later I still hadn't seen any Daltons, and started to relax. I'd kept busy though; besides doing my park chores, I'd built a little camper on the back of my truck, mostly out of free wood pallets from behind a lumber store. I traded in my cowboy duds for shorts, T-shirts, sandals, and a straw hat. I even caught fish. Not real big, or any great numbers of fish, but enough Spanish mackerel to warrant another trip to the lumber store for more pallets to build a smoker. So I was smoking mackerel and handing out samples to the folks in the campground.

Most evenings a few of us sat around a bonfire telling stories and having a drink or two. One night, after the other folks had gone on to bed, eighty-year-old Gus from Michigan came up with a jar of genuine moonshine. So we sat there in the dark where the bonfire had burned down, commenting on the various and sundry attributes of corn liquor and life. When Gus finally started running low on stories about himself and his wife traveling around, he asked how I ended up in the Sunshine State. I condensed my last long years of living in Texas into a few short minutes' narrative between nips of 'shine before going for the wrap-up.

"I decided since about all I got to show for them years of hard work possum ranching is a pick-up truck and a somewhat better vocabulary from doing so many cross-words, I might as well try something I always been wanting to do, like big-time saltwater fishing." Gus grunted either an agreement or a desire to hold the jar. I passed the 'shine and continued.

"Remember that show used to be on TV with that fella traveling around the country looking for the Ultimate Fishing Experience? That's kinda what I was thinking. What got me in mind to head this way first was finding an old road map of Florida laying on the seat of my truck. Found it there the same day the sheriff told us we had to leave. Never did figure out where it came from." I took the offered jar for a meditative slash.

"That, and I'm trying to avoid any kind of close personal contact with some folks known back home as the Dalton Gang." I took Gus's silence as a sign of his keen interest.

"They're a bad lot all right, them Dalton's. It ain't so much Lenny, but George's meaner'n a snake in a shook bucket. Luckily there's just the two of 'em, so it's not really much of a gang, though Lenny's big enough to make two of most men."

Gus started making little snoring noises, so I helped him back to his RV so he wouldn't do a header into the bonfire coals and wake everybody up screaming and hollering, all on fire and everything.

With Gus tucked safely away, I took it upon myself to finish the rest of the jar of White Lightning lest someone accuse me of being a social drinker. I got a vague memory of sometime between when I was talking with Gus and sunrise, standing in the surf with my fishing pole making long casts and singing ol' possum rancher songs.

* * *

After I had sufficiently recovered the next day, I caught more fish for the smoker. I gave the lady running the park some of the smoked fish and told her it was time for me to be moving on, since there was still a whole lot of Florida for me to see. She said she hated to see me go so soon, since I had been a big help to her around the park, and slipped me a little extra money for gas. She had a question too.

"Helping you with those crossword puzzles while you've been here has got me doing them now." She gave me a frown, but her eyes were smiling. "I got a question for you before you go. What's a six-letter word for 'small messenger or gift'? Doesn't make much sense to me, but it starts with an i, third letter is d."

I worked that a little. Didn't sound right to me either. "How about Indian?"

"It fits all right." She shrugged and wrote it in.

I saved some of the cooked fish for eating on the road and handed out the rest to my new friends there in the park. When word got out that I was leaving, they wouldn't take no for an answer and paid me for the fish. Since I was leaving the smoker there, I put Gus in charge and told him about the marinating and seasoning. We shook hands all around that evening, and I got to bed at a decent hour for once so I could get an early start for the East Coast.

* * *

I slept good that night in my little homemade truck camper, overslept a little in fact. It was a sharp metallic click that woke me up finally. I had a bad feeling about that click, and real slowly opened one eye.

"Morning, Taco Bob! Looks like it's going to be a nice day! Too bad you won't be getting to see none of it!"

Looking up the barrel of the large-caliber handgun pointed at my nose, I had far too good a view of the crooked grin of George Dalton. I went ahead and opened the other eye, then noticed Lenny standing outside looking around in the early morning light.

"Morning, George. You wouldn't shoot an unarmed man in his own bed, would you?"

"I don't see why not! I been waiting five years for this, so you'll excuse me if I savor this magical moment here just a bit before I blow your head off." I could see Lenny looking in, all anxious. The man was big as a refrigerator and almost as smart.

"Hey George, are we going to get us some breakfast? I shore am hungry." George pressed the barrel of the gun against my forehead and rolled his eyes.

"Lenny, I TOLD you we had to kill Taco Bob FIRST, then we'd get some breakfast! Remember?" I could see the bear-sized man outside looking embarrassed.

"Uh, okay George. I remember now."

George went back to giving me his full attention.

"The big dummy's got a point. This shooting people first thing in the morning does tend to make you hungry. Reckon I better get you shot so I can turn Lenny loose on a breakfast buffet somewheres."

George held the gun with both hands and closed his eyes, and I could see his trigger finger just a few inches away start to flex. I was close to soiling myself when I heard Lenny clear his throat.

"George! Hey, George, uh, I think we got company."

My executioner's eyes popped open and we could hear a squeaky voice coming up to the truck.

"Is Taco Bob still here? I thought he was leaving early this morning! You sure are a big thing! You like to try a strudel? That nice policeman who stops by here every morning can't eat too many because he's on a diet, so you can have a few."

While Gus's wife held up the pastry plate for Lenny, George was having second thoughts. Then we heard: "Oh, here comes that nice policeman now!"

George looked truly heartbroken; killing me obviously meant a lot to the man. I think there might have even been a tear in his eye just before he jumped out of the camper, grabbed Lenny by the collar, and high-tailed it out through the woods.

"What's wrong with them boys?"

It was the big cop that came around the park most mornings. He was sporting a sizable girth and a double handful of strudel. Little ol' Mrs. Gus stood there grinning, holding a big plate of her famous pastry. I didn't think it would do much good, but I mentioned it anyway.

"Morning, officer. That would be the infamous Dalton Gang; career criminals specializing in robbery, burglary, kidnapping, and extortion and most recently branching out into prison escaping."

"That so?"

I got the feeling the man didn't believe me. He seemed more concerned with selecting his next pastry off the platter than chasing dangerous felons.

I politely declined a strudel, slipped into my truck, and got out of there as fast as I could. I made sure I wasn't being followed by any Dalton Gangs, then aimed east for the oldest city in Florida.

Chapter 6

Charlie Spider

"Charlie's holding out, I just know he is!" Carol was obsessed. She paced the hardwood floor of her bedroom.

"He's got something going on he's not telling, and it's driving me crazy!" She picked up one of her notebooks and threw it on the bed.

"The man's been sneaking around for years. Making his secret phone calls, meeting shady people here at the mansion, or flying off someplace without telling us where he's going."

Carol inspected a well-chewed fingernail.

"These days all he does is act coy and say he's got plans, and all I do is walk around this freaking bedroom talking to myself!"

* * *

Carol had learned all she could about the man. There were notebooks full of information it had taken her years to collect. She knew more about the popular writer/guru than anyone. Not that that was a particularly good thing.

Charlie Spider had first made a name for himself in the
'70s with his series of books on the occult, sorcery, and
drugs. The release of the first books fit in well with the
fledgling New-Age movement, and the popular writer
fanned the flames of fame by remaining elusive and eva-
sive through the '80s while he continued to pump out
another book every few years. He got away from the drug
thing after the first couple books and was one of the first
to bring lucid dreaming out of the secret societies of the
mystics and onto the shelves of neighborhood bookstores.
His book *Dreaming for the Easily Led* gave some instruction on lucid dreaming mixed in with his usual fanciful
tales of magic and sorcery. It was his biggest seller. The
fact that it actually seemed to work a little made his grow-
ing legions of fans fiercely loyal to Charlie's books, and
overly forgiving of some obvious inconsistencies in his
stories.

Charlie was filthy rich by the time Carol moved into the
mansion in the late '90s. He had a worldwide following and
a big house full of young women he called Witchettes vying
for his attention. Then the workshop tours started.

Traveling around the country, then the world, appealed
to Carol. It was a little like hanging out with a rock band.
Actually a lot like it. Less music, but Charlie's talks with
some recycled stage magic thrown in drew good crowds. It
gave the women something to do, and Charlie got to audi-
tion a lot of prospective Witchettes.

Carol saw it all. While his books told of the powers available for the taking to anyone willing to live a life of absti-
nence, celibacy, and meditation, Charlie himself stayed busy
boinking plenty of nubile young culties and partying as hard
as humanly possible.

Then it happened. The man was at the height of his game, and promising big things to come, when his body suddenly gave out on him. Charlie melted like the Wicked Witch of the West in a matter of a few agonizing days. The rapid decline and excruciatingly painful death of the man who for decades had alluded to immortality in his books was kept from the press and public by the astonished Witch-ettes and a thoroughly stunned Carol.

"Charlie! How am I going to find out what you were up to now?"

* * *

"My God! I never dreamed he'd die! I just assumed he'd live forever!" Shasha seemed to be working herself into another crying jag.

Heather was still in deep denial. "Maybe he's not really dead. Maybe he's just traveling in the next dimension! I know he wouldn't leave us here alone!"

Several years of the good life with Charlie had left Carol with little tolerance for whiners and a few extra pounds. Unlike some women, when Carol gained weight, it went to all the right places. Even so, her initial pursuit of spiritual virtue had long ago been replaced by an ongoing quest to lose 5 pounds. She took the trembling and detestably slender Heather gently by the hand.

"Heather, honey, come with me."

They went for a private viewing of the famous guru's frosty, withered corpse jammed in the basement chest freezer. Heather ran off to her room, in full shriek. Carol shrugged.

Like the others, Carol was shocked that the old bird had checked out. But she was also pissed because not only would she never find out Charlie's secret, she was also going to have to start doing things more demanding than choosing lunch menus or taking long baths. It just wasn't fair.

Having to deal with the body hadn't been a barrel of laughs either. In fact, after Charlie started hanging out with the frozen pot pies, several of the women who helped Carol with the gruesome task cut out. Gretta, the former exotic dancer who had been with Charlie for years, said she was heading south. Nicki went back to live with her parents. Two others left without bothering to tell anyone where they were going. The remaining seven women got together for a strategy session.

"Maybe we should call Charlie's lawyer, see if there's a will."

Carol was the oldest at 29, and slightly more stable than the others.

"I do remember he mentioned something about a will once."

Sara had been with Charlie the longest. She spoke so rarely it got everyone's attention whenever she did.

"You know, one of the ways he controlled us was by never letting us have much money, he took care of all the financial stuff himself. I bet there's money hidden here in the mansion somewhere. I say we tear the place apart and find it!"

Sara had a wild look in her eyes none of the women had ever seen before. Carol thought of a caged animal sensing freedom.

"Good plan Sara, let's do it!"

The Witchettes started to fan out for the search when Heather spoke up.

"We can't do that! Charlie wouldn't want us snooping around like that!"

Six sets of eyes narrowed and stared at Heather. Carol put an arm around her fellow Witchette's shoulder.

"Heather, dear. Maybe you want to go down to the freezer and ask Charlie's permission first? No? How about you start with his bedroom, then, while I call the lawyer."

Finding a double fistful of hundreds under some sex toys in Charlie's sock drawer seemed to awaken some long dormant instincts in Heather. She organized and led the hunt afterwards. The library needed a meticulous search. The grounds needed to be dug. An attic. Basement.

Carol made an appointment with the lawyer, then gave Charlie's room another look. She went for the big piece of Mayan pottery that was Charlie's change jar. Easy enough to dump it on the bed. A few coins caught a good bounce and ended up on the floor. Never one to let any amount of easy money get away, Carol crawled under the bed and was trying to retrieve a dime from a crack in the floorboards when she realized one of the boards was loose.

"And what do we have here? Under your bed, dear Charlie?"

A loose board, then another. It took Carol a while to get all the stuff out of the secret compartment, but it was worth it. She had found what they were looking for. A manuscript for another book, stock certificates, photo albums of a lot of old Indians, stacks of crumbly little notebooks, an ancient-looking wooden pipe, small bags of dried God-knows-what, and a locked metal strongbox the size of a phone book. Carol slipped the box into her room and hid it under the mattress before she brought the other women to Charlie's room to check out the haul.

* * *

Dark. Creepy. Cold. After everyone was asleep that night, Carol snuck down to the basement and went through the pockets of Charlie's withered, frozen corpse and found the key. It took a couple of good belts of brandy back in her room before her hands stopped shaking enough so she could open the box.

Gold. Shiny. Warm. Though she had never seen them before, Carol knew what the two hand-sized gold idols wrapped in velvet were. Charlie talked about the Chacmools of the Ancient Ones at the workshops, but she assumed they were more of his metaphorical power-object bullshit. She didn't think they really existed. She was wrong.

The idols were solid gold and had a woman's head and what looked like an animal's body. Carol tried to remember what Charlie had said.

"When the Golden Chacmools are placed on the body of a dreamer, that person will be immediately transported to a world of infinite power and knowledge!"

Or maybe transported to a plane of the dream wisdom of the Ancients. Whatever it was, Carol was pretty sure Charlie said you needed three Chacmools to get off, and there were definitely only two in the box. The only thing else in there was one of those locking diaries, and Carol wasn't about to go digging through any more frozen dead people's pockets. Get some sleep, then cut the diary open in the morning. If they got screwed on the will, she could always sell the gold for some quick cash and cut town.

Carol held the heavy little idols, one in each hand. There's nothing like the look and feel of gold to bring a smile.

"I wonder where the third Chacmool is this very minute."

Chapter 7
St. Augustine Pays Off for Taco Bob
"Easy work and hard rocking!"

I wasn't always in mind to work on a fishing boat, but it seemed like a mighty good way to get some water under my feet and make some much-needed pocket money. The map I'd found mentioned Jacksonville and on south a ways had a lot of marinas, so that's where I headed.

I got into St. Augustine early afternoon, parked by a statue of an early Spanish explorer, and started in on one of my specialties — walking around and looking at stuff. There were some mighty nice boats in the marina, and I spent some time just taking in the sights. I got to talking to some fellas on one of the charter boats, and they told me about a boat that might be hiring on some crew. Things were looking good.

Headed over to the far end of the marina and found the boat all right, an older 36-foot Hatteras Sport Fisherman, the *No Quarter.* Didn't seem to be anyone around, but there was a Help Wanted sign on the dock.

"Hello! Anybody there?" As soon as I said that, a couple of eyes and a big nose surrounded by a generous amount of jet-black hair and beard popped out of the cabin door. The eyes squinted down, giving me a hard look. Fella had a real low, gravelly voice.

"Arrr! Who goes there? Friend er foe?"

"Friend, I reckon. Fella over the other side of the marina said I might could get a job here crewing for a day or two. Said to ask for Captain Black."

He was quick for a little fella with a bad limp. He moved kinda sideways like a crab, more of a scuttle than a walk. Was up on the dock giving me the eye head to toe and all around while I just stood there. Finally, he pulled himself up to his full height and squinted up into my face.

"So you want to do battle with the monsters of the deep, do ye? Crash through the towering seas and spit in the devil's eye?"

"Uh, well, I do need a job." I was beginning to think the man a bit peculiar. He hacked and spat, gave me another close-up squint.

"Ye got yer clothes on right side out, and ye ain't scratching like ye got the lice. Yer hired. Be here smartly, five a.m." Captain Black disappeared back in the cabin just as quick, leaving me wondering a few things. Like pay. But at least I had a job.

* * *

The next day was one to remember. The Jolly Roger flags on the boat and Captain Black dressed like a pirate during the job interview the day before should have tipped me off. I'd never heard of a Pirate Cruise before, but the Hendersons and Halls from Ontario had. Those folks told me they'd booked Captain Black over all the other charter-boats because of his pirate motif. So off we went for a day's fishing.

The Captain and his nephew Orville had on their pirate outfits and wasted no time getting wasted on rum on the way out. The Canadians thought it was great fun, those two drunk on their asses, shouting an impressive collection of seafaring obscenities to everyone aboard. Not having been out on a boat that big before, especially out of sight of land, it was a might disconcerting for yours truly seeing the people supposed to be running the boat stewed to the gills. It was not like me to be sober when there was an opportunity to be otherwise, but under the circumstances I elected to keep a clear head, just in case.

But my fears of shipwrecks and men overboard were thankfully unfounded. What actually happened in between all the pirate histrionics was some fine fish catching. Captain Black kept a bloodshot eye on his collection of electronic monitors while at the helm and called out orders.

"Thar she blows, Orville! We got bait clouds at ten fathoms! Man the port rods ye scurvy dogs!"

"Aye, ye old bastard! Cut 'er back some, we got fish ON!"

And Orville would grab a bent over rod with line screaming off the reel and hand it to one of the Canadians in the fighting chair before stumbling and falling hard. Each time the Captain would reverse engines at just the right moment to throw his inebriated kin off balance so he'd smack the deck. The Captain thought this was hilarious.

"Mind ye step, ye scallywag! Ye got sea legs like a girly!"

Which would send Orville raging into the cabin after his hysterical uncle. Then I would help the people with the fish, while those two threw vile curses and boat accessories at each other.

We landed several nice kingfish and even got one jump out of a big sailfish before starting back in. The day's fishing success was cause for breaking out even more rum, and we eventually found the right marina in the right town after only three tries.

Captain Black abandoned ship for the bars as soon as the *No Quarter* bumped into its home berth with Led Zeppelin blasting from the ship's loudspeakers.

"Ye sorry excuse for bilge rats be puttin' the knife to the fishes whilst I attend to the barroom wenches! Aye, it's a pirate's life for me!" And off he staggered down the dock with his sideways walk, pausing only to take a kick at a slow-moving dog or tourist. I went below to turn the music down and found Orville passed out on the floor of the cabin with his head in the head.

I did my best, cleaning and icing down the day's catch for our sunburned and wobbly clients before hosing down the boat and putting things back in some kind of order. The Canadians ended up all smiles and trucked on off with their fish after giving me a healthy tip.

The next day was more of the same with four folks from Dayton. Somehow, Orville and the Captain managed to get even more grog-bombed, but we caught fish again, and with my help coming in, we found the right marina on only the second try.

I got another nice tip that day, so I didn't too much mind the next morning when some weather moved in and a seriously hungover Captain Black informed me fishing was off for a few days. Orville was in his usual place on the floor, half inside the head, and the Captain seemed to be slowly

losing a battle with gravity over a plate of breakfast. I
wanted to thank the man for giving me a job and invaluable
fishing experience, but he was snoring in his grits before I
could get it said.

* * *

Since I was a bit concerned about my truck standing out
in a parking lot full of little rice-burner cars and SUVs, I'd
found a place to park in a secluded alley behind a fish
house. But I wasn't surprised to see the bottoms of some
very large boots sticking out from under my truck. I
approached cautiously, knowing where there's one Dalton,
there's soon two.

"Morning, Lenny."

"Morning, Taco Bob." I noticed a busted car jack under
the front bumper of my truck; Lenny was too big to fit under
otherwise. I took a look under at the unmoving Dalton.

"Lenny, I imagine that engine block resting on your forehead smarts a bit." I winced and looked again at the jack
that had given way.

"It's not bad, I had worse."

"So Lenny, I kinda got an idea already, but just to clear
things up for me, what is it you're doing under my truck?"

"Oh, nothing. Just cutting the brake lines, maybe a
bomb."

"I see. George around?"

"He run off to get another jack, get this motor off my
head. He should be back soon, then we're going to breakfast. I'm getting mighty hungry."

I noticed metal snips on the ground.

"You cut any brake lines yet, Lenny?"

"Nope."

"Bombs?"

"Nope. George has some hand grenades. Should blow up real good!"

"I'm sure. Look, Lenny, how about I get this truck off your head, and we call it off for today so you can get some breakfast?"

"Uh, yeah! You think that will be all right with George?"

"He's probably getting hungry himself by now. You just hold still while I unlock the truck here, get the jack out from behind the seat."

Thinking about George and hand grenades, I was able to get the truck jacked-up in record time. I started pulling the man-mountain out by the ankles.

"Damn if you ain't a mite heavy, Lenny!" I got him drug out, and while I was getting the truck down off the jack, that mass of humanity sat up rubbing on a greasy bolt imprint deep in his forehead.

"Thanks, Taco Bob. I was getting a bit of a headache there."

"Don't mention it Lenny. Be seeing ya."

I had hold of the doorhandle, about to make good a speedy departure, when I heard a metallic click on the pavement right behind me. Kinda like the sound you'd expect the pin from a hand grenade to make. My reflexes somehow judged the height and angle just right when I spun around with the jack handle, and caught a surprised George Dalton square in the side of the head.

As he went down, the grenade came loose. I dove after it, and did a scoop and throw any outfielder in the Big Leagues would have been proud of. I got to my feet, jumped in my truck and roared off just as the grenade went off under somebody's van.

Judging by the way George and Lenny were staring at the burning van as I went around the corner, I surmised it was theirs.

* * *

After a quick stop at a hardware store, I headed south along the coast and found a place to park for the night just the other side of a little town called Flagler Beach. Though I hated to do it, I spray-painted over the artwork on the sides of my truck. It had to be the reason they kept finding me.

I drifted off to sleep, listening to the surf from inside my truck camper, and had a dream about coconut trees and manatees. Try as I might though, I still couldn't remember to look at my hands in my dreams and count my fingers.

Chapter 8
Carol in Charge

Satellite trucks lurking outside the gate. The occasional hovering helicopter. Carol looked out a window across the manicured grounds of the Spider Estate and sighed.

"Somebody's going to have to face them, and I'm pretty sure I know who it is. Charlie's only three days gone, and already they've found out." She called a house meeting.

"Okay girls, the hyenas are at the gate and the vultures are circling." All eyes on Carol. She savored the moment, a new experience.

"Time to call a press conference."

* * *

The media was ravenous. Reporters licked their lips. Video cameras growled like empty stomachs. Micro-recorders waved in the air like hungry serpents. It was a slow news day the morning after a full moon, an often dangerous combination in journalism.

The tears were easy enough. Just thinking about all the work she would have to do to ensure a healthy cash flow for herself and the other Witchettes caused Carol genuine anguish. Underneath her drab cult clothes she could feel the little something she'd just bought. Something to keep her spirits up, as it were. Carol and the others had prepared a statement.

"Charlie Spider, spiritual beacon to thousands and pioneer on the path to the link with infinity, has gone on ahead."

Carol thought about how she was going to have to get up before noon everyday. A sob escaped. She held the statement notes lower to cover her other hand giving the concealed Frederick's silk a quick caress. She bravely pulled herself together.

"Though Charlie explored the mystery of awareness, the mystery of dreaming, and the ultimate mystery of mysticism, much work remains. A magical door has been left open. The Witchettes and I shall continue Charlie's legacy for those seekers who have read his inspiring and reasonably priced books, which are still available at better bookstores everywhere as well as online."

She conveniently failed to mention Charlie's legacy of party animal, and the fact that his biggest potential problem these days was freezer burn. Carol did fire up the faithful, though, with news of a soon-to-be-published last book of Charlie's called *More Dreams for the Easily Led*.

The press conference was an experience. All those anxious eyes staring intently. The media feeding on her words. Carol liked the almost sexual feeling of power. Of control.

*   *   *

Lawyers were another matter. The executor of Charlie's will was a well-practiced asshole. Carol expected trouble, but the Witchettes did all right in the will nonetheless. The mansion was theirs as long as they were in residence, and each of them would receive a small monthly allowance.

But the will stipulated that if they wanted any of the serious royalty money from the books, they were going to have to continue the workshops that had been so important to Charlie. Carol's ingrained reluctance to put out any more effort than absolutely necessary was swept away when she talked to the Spider Cult's accountant. The workshop tours had been knocking down some serious bucks.

The money and power thing. The power was something new, but Carol already knew what to do with money. She started getting the other women whipped into shape for giving lectures and running the lucrative T-shirt, book, and souvenir concession at the workshops while she explored the inner realms of self-awareness that could only be experienced in the boutiques and salons of Rodeo Drive. The new leader of the Spider Cult had several years' worth of repressed apparel-shopping issues that needed to be dealt with.

* * *

Charlie's handwriting was the worst, so it took Carol a while to figure out the story of the Chacmools. The little diary contained a lot of information though, and even mentioned a little bonus sorcery trick. Carol read her benefactor's words.

"The Chacmools of the Ancients are the Key to the Last Gate of Dreaming. According to legend, anyone who has mastered lucid dreaming can lie on their back and place a Chacmool by each ear, then take the third and place it inverted over the eyes. When the dreamer enters into lucid dreams, they will be guided by the three Chacmools.

"This person would have control over the dreams as in a normal lucid dream, except with the Chacmools' guidance, the dreams would not be a fantasy world, they would be real and affect the everyday world of waking consciousness and the people in it."

She couldn't help but think about the possibilities. To steady her nerves, Carol decided to answer the call of the Bavarian chocolate sampler that had followed her home from the last trip to Rodeo Drive.

"This is some serious shit, the big thing he said was coming. One more Chacmool and dear old Charlie could have done anything he wanted."

The diary went on to say that the two golden idols that went by the ears had open mouths and closed eyes. The one that covered the eyes and fit over the bridge of the nose had a closed mouth but open eyes. Carol checked her two idols. Both had open mouths.

Nibbling a delicate truffle, the new head of the Spider Cult tried to grasp the big picture. The money and power thing she had going on with the cult was shaping up nicely, but this!

"This rocks! I get my hands on a full set of these little idols, I can kick some ass! Literally!"

While pacing the room, she popped a mini bon-bon and thought about which asses would get kicked first. Start with some of those crooked politicians on television, maybe work up to some dictators.

"I could have the power of a queen!"

Carol issued an un-queen-like burp and went back to the truffles. She ate the whole thing in one bite and was blind-sided with guilt and self-doubt. She sat down hard.

"Who am I kidding here? I can't even lose five pounds. How am I going to find a lost ancient idol and rule the world, or even Westwood?"

But before she could slip too far into the void, Carol remembered the bonus sorcery trick.

* * *

The bonus: Instructions in the back of the diary for a technique called the "Black Eye." That was a nice sur-prise. Carol figured with all she'd been through, she was due.

After a few days of practice, Carol started getting the hang of it. It didn't always work, but she could sometimes mesmerize others into doing her bidding if she could get them to look long enough into her left eye, the one with the black contact lens.

Though it seemed the dim-witted were the most suscep-tible, the trick gave Carol's confidence a much-needed boost. She would quest for the third idol, on her own if nec-essary, as soon as she took care of some business. Then she just had to figure out where to look.

One of the people the Black Eye definitely wasn't going to work on was Wesley S. McGreed, the lawyer for the will. Though the executing of the will had turned into a long, drawn-out affair, Carol and the lawyer wasted no time devel-oping an intense dislike for each other. McGreed looked like a prime example of all the really bad things too much money could do to a person. She really hated the trips to his lavish office.

"You'll see, my dear, toward the bottom of that page a provision concerning Mr. Spider's nephew."

Carol didn't like the sneering smile she saw across the table. It had to be something really bad to be giving the lecherous old fart such pleasure. She found the place in the will and tried to decipher the lawyer legalese.

"We have to give him a job? Is that what all this means? What does 'until the first party is rendered non-resonant' mean?"

McGreed gave Carol an impatient look.

"It means, my dear, that you have to gainfully employ Mr. Jeremy Donner, for life."

Carol hadn't ever met Charlie's nephew, but this didn't sound good at all.

"Judging by the twisted little smile on your face, McGreed, I'm guessing it would be safe to assume the guy's a real loser."

The old buzzard had the creepiest laugh she'd ever heard.

*   *   *

Wal-Mart. Retail hell. Carol thought she was going to die. Jeremy stood right where she'd been told she'd find him, though. A greeter just inside the front door of the most bottom-end Wal-Mart in the country, conveniently located in one of the parts of LA best known for its riots.

Worried about what being seen in a place that far down the shopping food-chain might do to her reputation, Carol prepared for her journey into the armpit of retail with a blonde wig and sunglasses. She slipped inside the store unnoticed by following a group of giggling high school cheerleaders, and found a suitable place to observe

Jeremy in action. The man had no style, or looks for that matter. Balding already, going to fat. No family resemblance with Charlie, not even close. The only similarity seemed to be they were both short, and judging by the obvious way Jeremy was checking out the women as they came in the store, he was just as much a horndog as his uncle.

* * *

Witchettes, workshops, lawyers, accountants, and then several employees. Carol was a busy girl. She hardly had time to read more of the diary in between shopping excursions. But there was something very important she needed to know, and her heart sank when she finally got through the last page. It wasn't there.

"This sucks, Charlie! I need to know where to find the third Chacmool!" Yelling didn't help. She tried throwing the diary against the wall. That didn't help either.

Next, the CEO of Spider Cult International worked up a good case of self-pity and threw herself on the bed. Crying made her hungry, so she popped a handful of Bavarian Delights. Then a little more crying before wiping tears and chocolate off with the bedspread.

"Charlie was such an anal old bastard, he would have written down everything he knew about the third idol. It's got to be here somewhere."

Carol allowed herself a good belch, then dug out the metal box with the idols for another look, but there were no false bottoms or secret compartments. She went for the diary on the floor.

"Come on Charlie, you knew what that third Chacmool could do. I know you had to be looking for it!"

Some careful work with a knife, dissecting the cloth covers of the diary, didn't reveal squat. No microfilm, bus station locker keys, or coded messages. Nothing but blank
cardboard inside. Nothing.

Carol was ready to board Bavarian Cruise Lines for a
long, bloating voyage into the designer-chocolate sea of
despair. She still had the knife in her hand and stared at the
diary laying on the bed, its covers slit and peeled back
obscenely. She had checked everything, everything except
the thin little spine.

Just a sliver of onionskin paper was all that showed at
first.

Chapter 9

The Last Chance Trailer Park

Crickets in the night. A light breeze. An almost full moon rising above the trees as the front door of a trailer burst open and a very young woman in an extremely short dress stepped out and screamed back inside, "Fok you, you foking pervert!!! Dat ez de mose desgusteng foking theng I ever foking hear of!!!"

She slammed the door hard and marched over to the dusty, deserted road alongside the mobile home park and stuck out her thumb. Immediately, an old Chevy full of dark male faces appeared out of nowhere, picked her up, and was gone.

Jeremy Donner, head of shipping and receiving for the Spider Cult's T-shirt division, and former part-time greeter at Wal-Mart, lay on the floor of his dimly lit trailer in a pool of vomit and tequila. As he slowly pulled himself into a sitting position, he rubbed the welt on his forehead recently delivered by the Vaseline-covered baseball bat lying next to him on the floor. Jeremy could hardly speak.

"Maaaaan that hurts! I swear, if I live to be a hundred, I'll never understand women!"

He found a half-full bottle of tequila, took a slug, and shook his head like a wet dog before wiping his face on a dirty towel. A devilish smile appeared below hooded eyes; he'd obviously decided he wasn't nearly drunk enough yet and still wanted to party.

The little man looked around the room through the debris from his latest week-long bender until he found the phone and a business card. But before he could hit the number for Murray's Dial-A-Ho, there was a flash of lightning, the lights flickered off, the phone rang once, and the front door slowly opened.

* * *

A curvaceous form in a black lace teddy with black cape, fishnet stockings, and riding boots stood in the doorway, silhouetted by a lone streetlight. Carol had been practicing her entrances.

"Trick or treat!"

She glared at the pathetic figure cowering on the floor of the trailer before her. A wicked, knowing smile on her face, Carol was holding a roll of duct tape and a riding crop in her right hand, which she slowly tapped against a shapely thigh. Her other hand absently scratched an ample ass-cheek, where the silk teddy was giving her a rash. Jeremy sat speechless, a look of stark fear and sheer animal lust on his face. Carol stepped into the trashed trailer, grabbed him by the hair on the back of his head, and dragged him to the coffee table next to the couch.

"Let's get this show on the road. I've got a party to go to, but I need to take care of this first."

Carol slammed Jeremy's head down on the low table, and wrapped a generous amount of duct tape around both his head and the corner of the table. With his head securely fastened facing the couch, she wrapped his hands and feet as well, then lit a candle sitting on the table. The head of the Spider Cult stood back and looked down at the wretched, moaning figure below her.

"Okay, listen up, loser, I'm only going to explain this to you once. Since we had to hire your sorry ass to work for us a few weeks ago, you've been nothing but trouble. I've got enough to deal with without having to go around and clean up your messes. Speaking of which, don't you ever clean this pigpen?"

Carol reached for a black lace hankie sticking out of her boot and dropped her little whip next to the couch. She bent over to pick it up, giving Jeremy a close-up of a lot of ass and a little bit of black silk. Jeremy started making a different kind of moaning noise.

Carol straightened up, saw the look in his eyes, and gave him a pop with the whip. "No way, hotshot! This is prime stuff here!" She gave herself a little pat on the ass. "I'm saving this for the large number of tall, handsome, and well-endowed hotties I expect to meet on very favorable terms in the near future."

Carol sneezed from the dust and held the hankie to her nose.

"Which brings me to the point of our little get-together, loser. You're always after me to teach you how to do the Black Eye, correct?"

Jeremy's eyes got big and he started nodding his head. Carol sat down on a relatively clean part of the couch, leaned in close, and closed her right eye.

"Well, if you make a run down to Florida and find a certain little statue that I would very much like to have, maybe I'll teach you. How about it?"

Chapter 10

Jeremy Hits the Road

Jeremy just knew it was something bad. He was less than an hour out of LA, doing his best to keep up with traffic in his blue Pinto with the one red door, when the noise started. It was just a small scraping noise at first, which seemed to be coming from the front of the car. After first worrying himself into a sweat, Jeremy slipped into denial.

"Hey, no problem, these older classic cars got all kinds of little noises, it's part of their charm!" The noise started to get louder, so Jeremy turned up the radio.

An hour later Jeremy had put little balls of tissue in his ears and the radio blared at full distort. He noticed people in other cars were starting to stare and sometimes point at the front of his car when they went around. Jeremy finally pulled into a rest stop with the Pinto sounding like a thousand fingernails dragging on the world's biggest blackboard. The rest stop was doing a big business, and everyone in the place stared at the little car pulling in.

Too embarrassed to stop, Jeremy screeched the Pinto on through the rest stop, then another quarter-mile down the shoulder of the road before stopping. He casually got out and stretched, scratched himself, issued a manly belch, and gave a cautious test kick to the smoking left front wheel.

"Probably just a little hot, nothing to worry about."

After a much needed trip to the bushes, Jeremy checked himself out in the hand mirror he always carried, and as usual, he liked what he saw. He combed a few strands of hair over the vast expanse of barren real estate on top of his head. The mirror reflected Danny DeVito, but Jeremy's eyes saw Brad Pitt.

"Looking good! Hey, might be getting a little light on top, but maybe workout a little, lose a few pounds, and I'll be ready to read for the remake of Fight Club!"

Jeremy came out of the bushes and saw a small pair of legs sticking out from under the front of the Pinto. He hurried over to give whoever was obviously doing something bad to his car a solid kick. Just as he was about to deliver a good one to a skinny leg with his pointy-toed cowboy boots, the leg moved out of range and a little brown Indian kid popped out holding a wad of twisted rusty wire in his right hand.

"Hey mister! Here's the problem! You must have picked up this road trash, and it got wedged in against the wheel and the brake lining! Amazing this could make so much noise!"

Jeremy looked at the grinning kid holding up the rusty wire and wondered where he came from. There wasn't anyone or anything else around.

"Yeah, great, kid. You can keep it, okay?" Jeremy got in the car and pulled back into traffic. He looked in the rearview mirror, but the kid was gone. Lighting a cigarette, he told himself he knew it was just some wire or something all along and started rummaging around in the pile of stuff on the front seat looking for the map.

"Look out Florida! Here I come!"

Chapter 11

Taco Bob's First Trip
to the Everglades

"This sure don't look like Miami."

I left out of Flagler Beach early and drove on down south thinking about checking on Miami. I stopped at a little roadside fruit stand and bought a mango and some guavas, and started to ask the old Indian fella working there the best way to get to Miami. This little Indian kid popped up out of nowhere and didn't hesitate, told me right off like he was used to giving directions. So off I went.

By the time I checked the map to see what had become of the Greater Miami Area, I realized I had somehow missed it altogether and was out in the Everglades. I decided I'd catch Miami another time and just kept going on south through the Glades.

It was something like I'd never seen before, and it got me wondering how life must have been for those early Indians living down there in that part of the state folks called the River of Grass. Nothing for a hell of a lot of miles but grassy swamp and hardwood hammocks.

I stopped a couple times and looked out over all that wild country, then after dark I pulled into a little ol' bar off the main road a ways. I had me a bite to eat and a couple beers while talking with some of the folks living around there. Besides the universal conversations pertaining to matters of women, sports, and gas mileage, the beer talk that evening was airboats, fishing, gators, swamp buggies, and who shot what where last hunting season.

Later on, I pulled my truck over behind the bar and climbed in back to get a little sleep. I had my flashlight looking for a crossword to do to help me get to sleep and found a worn little booklet, a guidebook to the Keys and Key West. I thought over how it got there a while, then read myself to sleep.

I got a couple hours sleep, then lay there listening to the skeeters through the window screen for a few minutes before deciding to get my lazy ass up and head south some more before I ended up on the receiving end of another impromptu Dalton visit.

There wasn't a whole lot of Florida left down south to see, but I had a feeling it was the best part.

Chapter 12

Highway Irregularity

By the time Jeremy got into Florida, he was really sick of driving. It was getting hot during the day, and he hadn't slept well the last couple of nights in motels. The lack of exercise coupled with his diet of greasy roadside fast food had given him a serious case of constipation.

Now he was lost after trying a shortcut. Not lost enough to pull into a gas station and ask directions, but lost enough to maybe ask the two guys standing alongside the road.

"Yo, Chief! How do I get back on the interstate from here?" Actually, only one guy was standing up, the other one was the same height, sitting down.

"Get in Lenny!"

Jeremy hadn't planned on giving these guys a ride, just ask a quick question; but the big one was squeezing into the back seat before he could say anything. The other guy jumped in the front and gave him a hard look.

"Drive!"

Jeremy hit the gas, and the guy in front stopped staring at him long enough to look at the map.

"Take the next right."

"That's the way to the interstate? You sure?"

The guy kept staring at him, not saying anything. He looked up in the mirror and saw the big one in back just sitting there with a blank look on his face. This sucked.

"Where you guys headed? I'm not going much further myself."

"We're going to Miami. You're taking us."

Jeremy didn't like the way the conversation was headed, or the way the guy with the bruise on the side of his head kept staring at him. Maybe he'd try to lighten things up a little.

"Uh, sure, no problem. I hear Miami is nice; beaches, palm trees, that kind of stuff." These guys didn't look like your typical beach goers though. "I bet they got a lot of bars in Miami, topless bars especially." That was more like it, the guy turned the volume down a few notches on his stare.

"Pull over here!"

Jeremy almost missed the turn for the liquor store.

"Wait here, Lenny. If he moves before I get back, reach over and break his neck."

Jeremy hoped the guy was just getting a six-pack. The one filling up the whole back seat of the Pinto was staring at him now and looked like he was about to say something.

"Excuse me, mister, you haven't seen a white pickup truck with a big possum painted all the way down each side, have you?"

Before Jeremy could answer, there was a gunshot inside the liquor store, and the other man ran out and jumped in the car.

"Go!"

Jeremy kicked the Pinto hard, and they were back on the highway, the Pinto maxed out at seventy-five.

"Ease up, Mr. California, we don't want to draw attention to ourselves."

He must have seen the license tag. At least the guy was smiling now, looking down in the bag he got from the liquor store.

"Here you go Lenny." A handful of candy bars went in back. "They didn't have Mars, sorry."

"But George, you know I like Mars best!" Sounded like the monster in back was about to cry over a candy bar.

"Look, Lenny, I TOLD you they didn't have 'em! I even asked the guy. Explained it was important. When he said he didn't have any, I shot him, okay?" This was getting too weird for Jeremy.

"You just killed a man because he didn't have the right candy?" Jeremy glanced away from the road at the guy, who just gave him a look.

"Of course not! What do you think I am, crazy? I just shot him in the leg."

It sounded like a pack of hogs was eating the candy bars in back. George pulled a liquor bottle and a wad of money out of the bag.

"You mentioning them titty bars in Miami reminded me we're a little low on cash since we had a problem with our van and lost all our stuff."

Jeremy wasn't going to ask. He kept looking in the rearview mirror expecting to see police any minute.

"Lenny and me are going to get us a stake one of these days, settle down, maybe right here in Florida. Ain't that right Lenny?"

"Yeah, George! We're going to get a place of our own, like a farm! Tell him about the rabbits, George!"

"Nah, This guy don't look like he wants to hear about no rabbits." George was taking hits right out of the bottle and counting money. At least he seemed to be in a better mood.

"No, I like rabbits, really!" Jeremy had to lose these guys somehow. "Having your own place sounds great. So, you're going to do that in Miami?"

They were on the Interstate, heading south. At least there weren't any liquor stores on the Interstate. George got his dark look again, gritting his teeth.

"First, though, we got to kill a man."

Somehow, this didn't surprise Jeremy.

"Anyone in particular?" Jeremy chanced another glance over, and was getting that incredulous look again.

"Of course it's someone in particular! You think we're crazy?"

George belched and threw the empty bottle out the window. Jeremy had never seen anyone drink an entire quart of whiskey so fast.

"Man needs killing, too. Sent us up to the big house for five years!"

"Jeez! You guys are going to kill a judge?"

"Judge? Shit no! The judge is our uncle, or we mighta got even more time!" George pulled out a gun and waved it around. "Hells' bells, how were we supposed to know all them places we robbed had cameras up taking pictures!"

Jeremy saw a roadsign.

"Anyone need to take one? Next reststop after this is twenty-nine miles."

"You gotta go Lenny? Tell me now!"

"No, George."

The smaller man looked back and pointed the gun at Lenny.

"Don't be telling me in no ten minutes you gotta go!"

"I ain't gotta go, George, I'm sure."

George stuck the gun back in his pants.

"Maybe you better pull in here so I can bleed the lizard."

As soon as George weaved off into the restroom, Jeremy hit the gas. The car moved about twenty feet before there was an iron grip on his throat.

"Mister! We gotta wait for George!"

Jeremy hit the brake. He could barely talk.

"I seen a bunny up there! Under that red car, a little bunny rabbit!"

The grip eased.

"Where? I don't see it!"

"It's there behind the front wheel! If somebody doesn't get it, it might get splattered by a truck!"

Lenny worked his way out of the car just as George came out of the restroom pulling his gun. Jeremy credited George missing with all eight shots to the fact he was shitfaced and couldn't get a clear shot through the cloud of black smoke pouring out of the straining Pinto's tailpipe.

* * *

Jeremy decided the Everglades area at the bottom of the state had to be the biggest bore he'd seen since the desert, nothing but mile after mile of swamp. Hardly even any good billboards to read.

At least when he got to the Keys, there were bridges and water to look at; but through all the restaurants, dive shops, motels, mini-malls, and bait shops, he didn't see a single topless bar. There did seem to be plenty of bars though, and with the Visa gold card Carol had given him, Jeremy was sure he could find some action once he got to Key West.

It was a pleasant but cloudy day, and there were plenty of boats on the water around the bridges. If he hadn't been so constipated, Jeremy might have even enjoyed looking out over the water as he drove along. Finally, there was a break in the clouds and the sun came out, so Jeremy was fumbling around for his sunglasses and almost didn't see the young woman in the bikini standing on the bow of one of the boats. After that, the little man from California went on Code Red Cooter Lookout. Crossing Sugarloaf Key, he was checking out two college girls on a scooter, and didn't notice the armadillo crossing the road until it was too late.

"Jeez! I thought those things only came out at night!"

Soon afterwards, Jeremy started hearing deep rumbling noises and thought maybe the armadillo had messed up something underneath the Pinto. He turned the radio down and realized the rumbling was coming from his intestines. Maybe it was the mango he'd bought from that old Indian guy next to the gas station. Jeremy usually didn't eat fruit, but this guy was peeling the mangos and putting a stick in the end so you could eat it like a big lollipop. It actually wasn't bad, for fruit.

Jeremy hoped he could hold it till Key West. Get himself a motel room so he could take a nice, long, relaxing crap before getting this little statue thing Carol was so worked up about.

Chapter 13

Taco Bob Sees the Keys

*"All that clear blue water is near,
I could live on conch fritters and beer."*

Driving down toward the bottom of the state, the air changed about the same time I caught the first glimpse of water through the mangroves, and I started getting anxious to see what was up ahead. It was early morning by the time I hit the first couple of islands, the sun up enough I could get a good look at all the businesses and houses along the road of the upper Keys. It really didn't look all that different from the rest of Florida. There wasn't a whole lot of water to see down through Key Largo, but pretty soon there was plenty.

I never seen such beautiful clear water before. The sky was cloudy at first, but the sun started peeking out just as I was getting to some really nice areas, and you could see all the different colors in the water from up on the bridges. I hadn't ever realized there were so many different shades of blue and green.

By the lower Keys, the buildings, signs, and people thinned out some. There was more wilderness areas along the smaller islands, with a whole 'nother world of water out beyond.

I was easing down the road, listening to a Key West radio station, working on some smoked kingfish from a Vaca Key fishhouse, and taking in the sights. I was set.

A little blue car up ahead run over something on the road, so I slowed down and looked as I went by, and sure as hell it was an armadillo. I happened to look in my rear view mirror and seen what looked like a tall fella wearing a shower cap and some kind of skirt, run out, grab the 'diller, and run back in the bushes. Just up ahead, an old station wagon along the road had a sign for Chicken Burritos, but there wasn't anyone there.

I stopped at a State Park on one of the Keys, put on my swim trunks, and went and just lay there in that warm, crystal-clear seawater for a while. There was a few other people at the beach swimming too, and I talked to a couple from Toronto who seemed just as happy to be there in the bright sunshine and warm water as I was.

After a long swim I went over to the showers, got cleaned up real good, and got on the road without a single, homicidal Dalton popping up. I thought maybe my luck was changing for the better as I made for Key West at an easy cruise.

Chapter 14
The First Motel in Key West

The Chan brothers, who'd made a fortune in the laundry and illegal-immigrant-smuggling businesses, owned the first motel entering Key West. Using the same business strategy of packing as many desperate people in the holds of rusting derelict freighters as possible, the Chans bought several motels in Florida and remodeled.

The idea was simplicity itself. Just take an ordinary room, throw up some extra walls, doors, and plumbing and you have three rooms instead of one. It was not unlike what many movie theaters across the country had been doing for years.

* * *

"Hey, how ya doing? I don't have a reservation, but I got this and I need a room, like pronto."

André, the self-assured assistant manager of Big Pelican Nice Lucky Motel, looked up from his computer screen behind the counter and did a quick assessment of the short, pudgy, balding guy holding a Visa gold card up in his face like it was the Hope Diamond.

Oh joy, thought André, another asshole.

"I see. Let me just take a look at our room availability index." André sighed and looked back at the screen and tapped a few keys. The guy was sweating and fidgeting like crazy.

"Look sport, I'm in a big hurry here. I gotta take a wicked crap, so just take the card and give me the room key. I'll come back later and sign in and get the card."

André frowned, "I'm sorry sir, policy doesn't permit me to —"

"Look, would another twenty bucks on the card make policy happy? Thirty?"

The little man snatched the key André dangled over the counter and waddled back out the door of the tiny office as fast as safely possible.

"Welcome to Key West, sir!" André allowed himself a little chuckle as he ran the credit card through the machine. He was sure room 325-C was the farthest back in the motel, but he wasn't sure if the maintenance man had fixed that sticking door lock yet.

Chapter 15

Carol

Carol was pissed. Now instead of flying down to Key West to get her justly deserved third idol, she had to go to Germany to bail out the Witchettes. Sara called, whining about being up all night with the flu, said she was too weak to lead the other Witchettes in tonight's seminar. So Carol's rendezvous with destiny, her opportunity to wield unlimited power over all she encountered, was going to have to wait. This sucked.

Carol booked a seat on the next flight to Bonn so she could make one of her rare on-stage appearances. Germany sounded beyond boring.

"If we're going to take this Dog and Pony Show all the way to Europe, we should at least make it someplace with decent shopping, like Paris."

And speaking of sick and whining, Jeremy had called complaining about getting food poisoning in some big swamp somewhere in south Florida. He'd spent three hours on the toilet in a motel in Key West. That was the good news.

The bad news was his old car wouldn't start, and he wanted to head for the bars to unwind from his long drive. Since the little weasel could easily "unwind" for a week straight rather than going to the Treasure Museum like he was supposed to, Carol nixed that idea. She gave him an earfull, including the usual threats of losing his employment and genitalia, and finally told him to get with the program or she'd put a stop on his credit card.

The thought of being stuck in the opposite end of the country with no money seemed to get his attention. As much as she didn't like the idea, Carol realized she was going to have to depend on Jeremy to discreetly start gathering information on the treasure scene in the Florida Keys.

* * *

After packing for her trip to Germany, Carol had some time to kill before leaving for the airport, so she sat on her bed and read through the story of the Chacmools one more time.

According to Charlie, the Chacmool idols were from the Ancient Toltecs of Mexico. Seems the Spanish had paid the Toltecs one of their little visits that were so popular back in the 1600s and 1700s and grabbed everything of value, including two of the Chacmools. The third was hidden from the Spanish by a shaman who'd passed it down through generations of shamans until Charlie picked it up from an old Indian in a small town market in central Mexico for two hundred dollars cash and a carton of Marlboros. The old Indian told Charlie the story of the Chacmools and the power they could hold if all three were together.

It was another twenty years before Charlie had the second Chacmool. It cost him over a hundred thousand dollars to have it stolen from a museum in Spain. Several more years of searching Europe's museums and private collections failed to turn up any trace of the last idol.

The last entry was only weeks before Charlie's death. It said that the Spanish sailing fleet carrying the Treasure of the Ancient Toltecs back to Spain had run into a hurricane and lost a ship, the one most likely carrying the missing Chacmool. According to Charlie's diary, the ship had gone down somewhere around Key West.

Carol looked at her diamond watch and sighed. Time to head for the airport.

"All Jeremy has to do is find one little golden idol. Is that too much to ask?"

Chapter 16
Free Estimate

"The starter's shot, the battery won't take a charge, the alternator's fried, and the belts are disintegrating. The radiator and water pump are leaking, the plug wires are cracked, the wheel bearings are gone, the tires are past bald, the muffler is hanging by a thread, and there doesn't seem to be any oil in the engine."

The young Cuban mechanic looked up from his clipboard, "Do you want me to go on?"

Jeremy was no fool. He had this guy pegged as one of those con artists you heard about that ripped off tourists.

"No way, Chief! I just drove this car straight through from California without a bit of problems!" Jeremy didn't figure the wad of road-trash wire counted.

The young man seemed undaunted. "Whatever you say, sir. If you want us to do the work on your car, here's a preliminary estimate."

He tore off a copy from his clipboard, handed it to Jeremy, and drove off in a wrecker with palm trees painted on the side.

Jeremy looked at the estimate for $5,312.45, wadded it up and threw it on the front seat of the Pinto, which seemed to be listing to one side from a flat tire. He gave the car a good kick, and his boot toe stuck in a rusted-out hole in the door. While letting loose with a barrage of obscenities and struggling to get his boot unstuck, he felt something move in his insides. Jeremy stopped yelling, slowly pulled his boot out, and carefully waddled back up the two flights of stairs, hoping he wouldn't get a butt-cheek cramp before he got to the room.

Chapter 17
The End of the Road for Taco Bob
"Give me coconut trees and a warm ocean breeze!"

I drove on down A1A across all those islands and bridges, with that beautiful water going out in each direction as far as you could see, till I ran out of road. With a head full of information from the little guidebook, a light wallet, and an optimistic outlook, I arrived at the most famous island in the Florida Keys.

Key West ain't a real big place as far as islands go, only about a mile or so by four miles, but it's got a unique history and natural charm unlike any other place in the US.

On a map, the Keys is that line of islands coming off the bottom of the state that looks like Florida is taking a leak on Cuba. The islands are actually part of a long coral reef starting around Miami and going down past Key West. The part of the reef sticking above the water is the Keys, and the part just a few feet under the water around the Keys is what was making Key West one of the biggest and richest cities in the state at one time.

Way before the railroad or highway ever made it to the last big island, Key West was a happening place. Back in the early 1800s, big ships from all over the world trying to get through the Florida Straits would sometimes wreck out on the reef, and their cargo usually got hauled off real quick by the folks from Key West. This made for about every conceivable kind of people and merchandise of the period ending up on the little tropical island.

Lighthouses eventually put the wreckers out of business, and cigar makers from Cuba were the big news in town for years. The Navy came in and built a fort, then a big base that kept folks busy for a while. There were always fisherman and smugglers, and over the years there came to be a generous sampling of humanity living in everything from mansions to shacks.

These days the island is pretty well covered with all kinds of hotels and motels, restaurants, bars, museums, and every kind of shop you can think of for selling stuff to tourists. The big spot for the tourists is Duval Street in the section called Old Town, on the west end of the island. Duval ain't but about a mile long, but it's got the Atlantic Ocean on one end, and the Gulf of Mexico on the other.

* * *

While looking for a parking place, I got my first glimpse of some of the historic architecture going on in Key West that has survived the assorted hurricanes, tornadoes, and fires over the years. Some of the houses I saw looked like they got themselves fixed up these days even better than when they were new.

I found a place to park my truck on Duval next to a restaurant with seating outside and chickens running around on the ground. It reminded me of back home. I eased over toward an empty table with a view of the street out front.

"Just hit town, and right off snags one of the primo parking places on the whole island."

It was a waitress, a big woman with a big smile, wiping off a table next to the one I was heading for. I give her a nod and a smile back.

"As a matter of fact. How'd you —"

"The way you're looking around at everything for one, the guidebook in your hand for two, and I'm pretty sure I'd remember that truck of yours." She set a glass of ice water and a menu in front of me and continued.

"Too late for breakfast, but I can get you a sandwich. I'd recommend the grouper, or else the chicken. It's guaranteed fresh." That came with a big wink, and an on-cue confirmation from a couple of yard birds squawking and chasing along the fence.

"I'll take a chance on the grouper."

"Comes with a salad. I'm guessing ranch dressing. Be right back."

I had the little guidebook still in my hand. "How'd you know what this was?"

She turned her head on the way to the kitchen. "Hard not to recognize. I wrote it."

* * *

With my salad came an explanation. "I write about the Keys for a Miami paper once in a while. A few years back, I put some of my articles together for that little book. It's been out of print for a while, but I still see copies of it now and then."

I was impressed, and said so. She shrugged.

"I've done a lot of things since I landed on this rock thirty years ago. Besides waiting tables and writing, I've worked as a secretary, tended bar, and driven a cab. It's been a long time, and I may have put on a pound or two since then, but I even danced at the local strip club for a while." She grinned at my look, then started off toward another table shaking her head. "The stories I could tell you about that place!"

* * *

When my sandwich came, I was reading about Key West seceding from the union. Not at the start of the Civil War either, this happened back around 1982. I took advantage of the opportunity to inquire.

"That was a mess! The Feds blocked off the road into the Keys, said they were looking for drugs. Backed traffic up for miles. Lot of people around here said the government was screwing up tourism, so their solution to the problem was to declare war on the US, then immediately surrender and ask for financial aid. They finally got it worked out, and the flag of the Conch Republic is still a popular item in the gift shops around town."

The lunch crowd started getting serious, so I didn't get a chance for much more chat. I enjoyed my sandwich and read about Ernest Hemingway.

Seems Key West is fertile ground for those interested in learning about, or acting like, Hemingway. There's a nice house that used to belong to Old Papa hisself that you can visit, and a couple of the bars where he's supposed to have hung out are still here and do a lively business. There's even a Hemingway Look-Alike Contest every year that has a bigger draw of contestants than you might think.

I finished my lunch and sat back to let the world go by for a few minutes. In amongst the flow of wandering tourists passing by for my viewing pleasure was the occasional barefoot local on some purposeful mission. Mostly the chickens went about their business, but I did see a scrappy little rooster give chase to a man in shorts and cowboy boots once. After settling the bill and thanking the waitress, I headed out for a look around.

Though Hemingway died long before he could cash in on his popularity in Key West, Jimmy Buffett don't seem to be one to miss out. There's even a place called Margaritaville on Duval Street, so I just had to stick my head in the door. I was a little disappointed not to see anyone obviously wasting away in there; but it was still early, and I figured I'd check back again later on.

I eased on through the busy streets of Old Town just taking it all in. The tropical plants blooming, locals in shorts and T-shirts riding old bicycles, music and laughter coming out of the bars, food smells from the restaurants, the warm ocean breeze, and a big bright blue sky up above it all made for a feeling I decided I could get used to.

Chapter 18
Jeremy Homes in

Jeremy homed in on the lone topless bar in town like a testosterone-powered guided lust missile. Wearing a new Hawaiian shirt covered with bare-breasted hula-girls, shorts, and cowboy boots, he marched through town straight to the bar. His trajectory wavering only once when a chicken took offense to the sound his boots made as he hurryied along the sidewalk.

Once inside the dimly lit bar, Jeremy breathed deep the overwhelming aroma of mid-level tackiness that greeted him like an old friend. Like many such establishments, the owners had obviously decided long ago it was easier to keep the lights low than clean the place. Jeremy got comfortable on a sticky barstool and drank in the gaudy ambience and watered-down liquor.

After he'd attained a suitable glow, Carol's man-on-the-scene laid in a strategy. He decided he could learn more about treasure in Key West from talking to the locals than wasting his time hanging around some dusty old museum.

This might not have been a bad plan actually, except the only locals at the Pink Snapper Lounge that early were the bartender and bouncer, who both seemed to have a case of the black ass and didn't want to chat with the clientele.

Jeremy finally settled for a lengthy, rambling conversation concerning gas mileage with a couple of sunburned fisherman from Ohio, but the part of his brain that controlled speech shut down when the evening's first dancer hit the stage.

Chapter 19

Working the Tourists in Paradise — Taco Bob Makes a Friend

"Tired of the snow, but I know which way to go.
There's a place called the Florida Keys."

I took a walk down Charterboat Row and asked around to see if anybody was hiring, but nobody knew of anything right off. There wasn't much else to do except keep walking, so I did.

I wandered on over toward one of the beaches and there was a fella with long hair leaning on a handrail, throwing little bits of bread to the seagulls. Instead of flying around screeching and making a fuss like usual, the birds were all standing there patiently waiting for the crumbs.

"Don't think I ever seen them 'gulls come up so close like that before."

I settled in leaning on the railing next to the man myself, and checked out the bird show going on. The fella sighed and gave me a look with his big sunglasses. He was younger than me, maybe mid 30s, medium build, fine features, and a goatee beard.

"The birds, they trust me. I seem to have a way with animals; it is part of the curse."

Fella had a bit of an accent. He took off his sunglasses about the same time I noticed a couple of healthy-looking young women in swimsuits on the beach were looking rather intently our way. There ain't many men I seen that I'd call pretty, but this guy sure was, almost what you'd call effeminate.

"Well, it's good you got that thing with the animals going for you. The curse stuff don't sound all that good though." I gave those good-looking gals a smile and a little wink. There wasn't any response though; they weren't looking at me. The fella gave a good toss with some bread crumbs and let out a big sigh. He looked me square in the eye.

"You don't know the half of it, señor. You don't know what it's like knowing that you're destined to spend the last half of your life searching for something that most people think is just a fantasy, and a silly fantasy at that."

I gave that some thought while he was working on another of his big sighs.

"I might understand your situation there friend. I'm myself hoping to be spending a goodly portion of my remaining time alive in the here and now chasing after the Ultimate Fishing Experience." I was thinking about going into how I was also looking to eventually do some serious lucid dreaming, when he stuck his hand out for a shake.

"Juan Ponce, at your service, señor."

"Taco Bob's the name. Nice to meet you Mr. Ponce." We were into the handshake thing, and I was about to ask about his familiar-sounding name.

"Please call me Juan, Señor Bob. Some here call me Ponce de Gato because of my profession and my ancestry." He leaned down a little while he was talking, and there was a big orange cat appeared just in time for a quick brush with his fingertips. Cat was purring to beat the band. When I looked back again from the two women on the beach arguing, the cat was gone.

"Well then, Juan, I'd be proud if you just called me Taco. Hey, you ain't no relation to —"

"Yes, Señor Taco, I'm Juan Ponce de Leon the thirteenth direct descendent of the famous discoverer of Florida." This news was followed closely by his biggest sigh yet.

"You don't say? That's purty cool, Juan! I guess that has something to do with the curse then."

And it turns out it did. The man launched into telling me about how all those generations of Juan Ponces were always getting all eaten up with looking for the Fountain of Youth about the time they hit middle age.

"I can feel it coming over me now, Señor Taco. Every day when I look into the mirror and see a new gray hair, or a little line on my face, I know my destiny is drawing closer."

Juan was really taking this stuff hard. We both looked out over that timeless expanse of never-changing, always-changing sea before us, and each gave a good sigh. I seen the two young women were taking a break from giving Juan the eye, and appeared to be drawing straws.

"I reckon I know a little about where you're coming from there, Juan. Just about everybody got some of that going on when they reach a certain age, you know."

"Ah, but Señor Taco, for me it is in the blood! It comes over us Ponces and we become obsessed! We have carried the curse since the first Ponce came to the New World!"

I decided to try and change the subject, since this curse stuff was making the man sigh so much I was worried he might not be getting enough air.

I noticed the young women on the beach had stopped flipping a coin, and were rassling around in the sand. All the hair pulling and screaming they were doing had scared off the birds but was drawing a good crowd of gawkers. Juan gave the scene a bored look and there was another commotion started up behind us in the bushes.

A lizard came out of the bushes running up a palm trunk with three cats in hot pursuit. The cats hadn't got far up the tree when Juan looked that way and all three froze. Those cats kind of hung their heads and started backing down real slow like they knew they were in trouble. I seen Juan was giving them a look and shaking his head.

"Juan, you said folks called you Ponce de Gato? Seems like I remember Gato means cat; are those your cats there?"

The man came up with another sigh, but it didn't seem to be quite so life threatening this time.

"Yes, these naughty kitties here are some of my charges."

The three cats had come down from the tree. They were walking low to the ground, trying hard to look inconspicuous.

"They are part of our act, Señor Taco. We perform most days at the Mallory Sunset Dock for the people there."

One of the cats slinked over toward Juan's feet and flopped over on its back. Juan waited a bit, then gave the cat a brief brush on the belly with the toe of his shoe. Cat's purring sounded like a little boat motor.

"Well, that's cool. What kind of act you got going on there, Juan?" In my present financial predicament I was also wondering how good it paid, and if maybe I should be thinking about putting together a possum act or some-thing.

"The cats do some little tricks for the people." He snapped his fingers twice, and a cat I hadn't seen yet came out of the bushes and jumped straight up in the air, flipped, and landed on its feet. Then stood on its back legs and bowed. The cat's eyes were locked on Juan, who gave a lit-tle nod and the cat came over for a quick stroke on the back.

"Some of the others have little tricks, but mostly I juggle the cats."

Thus ended any thoughts of Taco Bob and His Trained Possums. Other than pretending to be asleep, possums didn't do much in the way of tricks, and I wasn't about to try juggling no possums.

The two young women had stopped wrestling around on the beach and the crowd had thinned out.

"I must go attend to some of my affairs, Señor Taco. Come by the Mallory Docks for sunset sometime if you want to see the little cats fly."

I told him I was looking forward to it, and he headed out with at least a dozen cats and one smiling, sandy-bottomed beach wrestler falling in step beside him. The other gal brought up the rear. She had their beach stuff, a puffy eye, and a slight limp.

*　*　*

There's a place down at the southern end of the island with a big concrete monument called the Southernmost Point in the Continental US. Lots of people around there tak-ing pictures of the marker and each other. Not too far away they were also taking pictures of one of the more unusual phenomena I seen in Key West.

There was a big fat guy there wearing gray clothes, and his skin and hair were colored the same shade of gray too. The man was set up under a big palm, playing a guitar and singing songs about coconut trees, the Florida Keys, and warm ocean breeze. For a minute there, I thought it was Marty the Manatee himself, but then I realized it was a Marty impersonator. The only person more famous in that part of the world than Hemingway or Buffett was Marty the Manatee.

Marty got his start years earlier in Key West when he first dressed up like a manatee and was playing in the bars around town. The man worked hard and got to be a damn good musician. Then he wrote the song that put a smile on the face of people across the country.

"Tequila Breakfast" became the anthem for folks everywhere dissatisfied with their jobs, lives, and local weather conditions. That song got a lot of people dreaming of a carefree life in the tropics: a life of warm breezes, porch swings, and cold beer. People flocked to Key West in droves on their vacations to try to live a bit of the dream and hear Marty, even a Marty impersonator, sing the song that had brought them there. I really couldn't blame 'em none either, because that song did have a bit to do with my own decision to check out Key West.

This was the first Marty the Manatee impersonator I seen, but not the last. I found out later that there were usually several Martys singing and playing guitar on the streets and in the bars of Key West.

The tourists were eating it up, and I thought this was a kind of ridiculous thing for a grown man to be doing, until I got a look at the kind of money this guy was getting in his tip bucket.

While again pondering on my own dismal financial situation, I wandered over by another of the little beaches and fishing piers. There was a young black fella, maybe 16, standing there wearing Stevie Wonder wraparound shades. He had a table set up with all kinds of little seashells and big conch shells to sell to the tourists.

Like everybody else he was wearing shorts, but his were real baggy and looked like they were slipping down real bad. His boxer shorts was hitched up to about his chest, and he was trying to get a spinning plate to balance on a stick while bopping around to music only he could hear on his headphones. I started to mention to him his britches were about to fall off, but he was really into the plate and stick thing, so I thought it might be better to let it pass.

I walked out the little pier, and the only one there in the afternoon sun was an old black fella wearing a big straw hat. He was leaned back good in a little fold-up chair, holding a fishing pole propped against the railing, and appeared to be asleep. I eased up quiet and looked down at the water where he was fishing and seen he not only didn't have any bait, but his hook was dangling about six inches above the water.

"Makes it more sporting for the fish, don't you know."

The old fella startled me. I looked over and seen one eye opened and some gold teeth showing under the hat.

"No doubt. I would imagine it makes for some rather light meals come suppertime though."

Now there were two eyes open and more gold teeth showing out of a smile.

"Ya, mon. I jus letting the lil fish get sure of themselves for now. They think the old man no good fisherman. I catch them later when I not working."

I couldn't help but look around to see what kind of work it was the old man thought he was doing. He nodded his head toward the young fella with the shells.

"Breaking in the new mon. Is my grandson, named Willie like me. I teaching him the family business, don't you know."

It was my turn to do some grinning, and Mr. Willie the Conch Shell Man and me did some hand shaking and introductions. I sat there with the old man for a while and spent some quality time listening to him tell me about seashells and the sea.

* * *

Come late afternoon I joined a lot of other people heading over to Mallory Square to catch the latest edition of the daily sunset. I reckon a lot of them people must not have sunsets where they come from, because it's like the main attraction of the day in Key West. There were all kinds of street-performer folks showed up doing mime stuff, some musicians and magicians, and Juan Ponce with his cat show.

Man could sure juggle cats all right. Those same fierce lizard-hunters I seen earlier would just curl up in a ball and let him throw 'em up in the air. Damnedest thing you ever saw.

The one young woman from the beach was there all smiles, having a good time helping with some of the tricks. I noticed the gal with the shiner was sitting off to the side, looking dejected and ignoring a couple of sailors who were clowning around trying to get her attention.

The sun finally set down into the ocean and everyone clapped, like they were maybe worried there could have been some other outcome to the day, and were just really happy that the sun did make it down all right.

The sun successfully completing its trip into the ocean for another day was also the signal for everyone to break ranks for the bars. I found a little place where it wasn't too crowded or too expensive and had another grouper sandwich and a couple beers myself. Of all the things I enjoyed about Key West, the best thing was it seemed to have far less Daltons than other places I'd visited in the state.

Chapter 20
Butch

When Butch came in at 9, Jose, the other bouncer, told him the little fat guy staring at the dancers with his mouth hanging open had been asking about treasure hunters.

Butch was 26, 6 foot 3 inches tall, and 230 pounds of muscle and arrogance. The New Jersey native watched wrestling on TV religiously and wore tight black T-shirts with pictures of wrestlers on the front. Butch had a big nose, long sideburns, and his dark hair combed like Elvis. He was big enough, young enough, dumb enough, and naturally mean enough not to be afraid of much of anything.

Except sharks. Butch had a mind-numbing fear of sharks that went back to when his parents took him to a drive-in movie in Tampa to see *Jaws* at a very young and impressionable age. They had parked in the front row.

Butch wouldn't go swimming, not even in the neighbor's backyard pool after that. Even as an adult he wouldn't go in a bathtub without checking under the soap bubbles first.

* * *

"So what's up with the yahoo and treasure? Fuck do I care?" Butch checked his hair in the window reflection by the front door.

"Before the talent showed, he was going on about how he was representing some big client who would pay some serious cash for a certain piece."

Jose pulled something out of the pocket of his jeans and stuck it in Butch's hand.

"And Cindy came by earlier and said to give you this."

Butch glanced at the packet in the semi-darkness of the bar.

"Shit! That bitch! This don't look like no $50 to me!"

"Be cool man. I already dipped a little, since we been smoking mine all week."

Butch gave Jose a hard look, but Jose just smiled and handed over a pack of rolling papers. "Your turn, amigo." Jose held eye contact and kept smiling. "Be sure to leave me half on the top shelf."

Butch gave Jose another round of hard looks and headed for the storeroom.

Chapter 21

The Wisdom of Grunts
Comes to Taco Bob

*"Those ain't exactly what first comes to mind
when I think of trophy fish."*

I found a place behind a little bakery there in Key West
to park my truck for the night. Nobody seemed to mind, but
I didn't get a whole lot of sleep. About the time the alley cats
finally stopped fighting and fussing, the first shift of roost-
ers started up.

In the morning I got myself a cup of coffee to go from
the bakery and drove over to the pier where I'd seen Mr.
Willie the day before.

Young Willie seemed to be just finishing up setting out
the seashells there on the table and on the ground in front.
With his arms folded, the old man was standing off to one
side scratching the gray stubble on his chin and watching
every move his grandson was making.

"Boy, I don't know why you always want to be putting them ol' Welks up on top like that! You got to turn them Queens so the color show better too!"

The kid didn't have his shades on and he was giving the old man dagger eyes, but he was moving some shells around. He glanced over at me and gave me the tiniest little wink.

"And don't be putting them Tritons like that! Why you do that? You got to pay attention, boy!"

There were more shells moved, and they finally seemed to be right for the old man.

"Pay attention to them customers better and don't be playing with your fool plates alla time neither!"

The boy didn't say anything, just sat on his little stool, slipped on his shades, and gave up a big grin like he was running for county commissioner or something. Mr. Willie narrowed his eyes and looked at his grinning grandson a few seconds then came over toward me. We walked out on the pier a ways before the old man stopped and looked back toward the seashell enterprise.

"That boy knows I hate to see him smile like that! Can't get him to argue with me like he should ought to! Does all that damn smiling just to get me upset, he does! Boy just too damn happy for his own good!"

Mr. Willie had his chair and fishing pole already out there. He'd told me the day before to bring my fishing stuff, and he'd show me some fish. He reached down in a bucket he had there covered with an old towel, and pulled out a wooden spoon with some yellow glop on it that looked like oatmeal. He tapped it on the railing so the stuff fell in the water.

"That be my special chum, now. The tides they good this morning, so we just have to wait a little while and I show you some fish!"

I had a seat on the pier and leaned back on the railing and closed my eyes. I let the morning breeze and the old man's stories wash over me while we waited for the fish to come.

"I don't always be the Conch Shell Man of Key West, you know. Spend most of my young-man days on the water. Man could do all right in them old days fishing.

"Soon as I was big enough to pull a anchor I be off on them boats. Them days the water around Bahama Islands and these Keys here, they all the fish and lobster and turtle you want. Not like these days, no; them days plenty for everyone. Water so clear you take the sponges from the bottom with a long pole, never have to go in the water for them."

The old man took a quick look down in the water and dropped in another spoonful of chum.

"I chase around many a year and learn me some things about the sea too. I got myself a wife for a while down by Freeport town, but the fever take her one spring. Enough years and my eyes, they aren't so good as they was, so I get a job here with a man sells these little shells.

"The man, he go and get himself sick, so I go into business for myself. Lots of tourist people want to buy shells, take them shells home to look at. By and by I saved me enough money, I get a little house here. And you know, as soon as I the businessman and property owner, I got my long-lost relatives, they all come showing up to visit."

Mr. Willie was smiling and gave me a wink.

"Yes sir, all kind be showing up here to visit since then. Just this last time, my daughter, she left off her boy Willie here. Boy got problems with his school, got his ass expelled for being trouble."

Young Willie was out of earshot, but he must have known something was up because he turned a little in his chair and glanced out toward us when his grandfather was talking about him.

"So now, these days I got a boy here I'm trying to learn the ways of the seashell business."

He didn't ever say what the boy had done to get kicked out of school, but I think it had more to do with attitude than any serious crimes against humanity. Mr. Willie would never come to admit it, but you could tell he cared a lot for the boy.

Every few minutes another spoonful of chum went in the water until finally the old man looked at the water and the sun, checked the breeze, and whispered so the fish wouldn't hear — that it was time.

He took a piece of the frozen shrimp I had bought on my way that morning, and after inspecting my hook and pronouncing it good enough, he had me baited and ready. I was directed on location, depth, proper body position, and how to feel for the right bite.

Within a couple of hours, Mr. Willie had turned me into a first-class grunt fisherman. I knew not only how to catch 'em, but the different kinds of grunts, the best way to clean 'em, and several interesting recipes for cooking the tasty hand-sized fish. The most unusual was "Stuffed Grunts," which is fried whole grunts stuffed with cheese grits. I was assured this was the best way to get a good dose of that most famous of all Key West dishes — Grits 'n' Grunts.

Mr. Willie said he already had brought a lunch for him and the boy, so I took my stack of grunt fillets and drove my truck over to a little park close by with picnic tables and grills. I got myself set up, and just as I was starting to cook,

I seen Juan Ponce and his feline entourage walking down the street. I gave him a yell to come over.

"Señor Taco, there is no doubt these are some fine-tasting grunts you have cooked here!"

I was proud my grunts were coming out so good. I was also hungry and was wasting no time putting away some fish myself while trying not to look at all those sets of sorrowful cat eyes staring up at me. I noticed the tallest, newest, and best built of Juan's following was absent. I inquired. Juan sighed.

"She has gone to the shops to buy new clothes for me. I told her that I have no need of fancy clothes because soon I will be off to the swamps and bog-lands of Florida to spend the rest of my life looking for something that might not even exist." He took a break for a quick sigh. "All my life there are women like this that want to do things for me. I think it is also part of the curse."

Before he could get too far into the deep sighing thing again, I had to ask.

"Juan, what with all those ancestors of yours looking around for the Fountain of Youth all those years, didn't none of 'em find anything?"

This seemed to brighten him up some.

"Yes indeed, they did find many things! The first Ponce, after he discovered Florida for the Spanish King, he spent all his time looking for the Fountain in the clear springs across the state. He found many wonderful things in nature, as did his son, and the next few generations as well."

We broke up the leftover fish into enough pieces to equal the number of sets of cat eyes that had been watching us eat.

"Ponce the Seventh was the first to go into the underground caves of Florida looking for the fountain. He too found many beautiful and wondrous sights, but no spring of eternal youth. Others have swum the lakes looking for springs, and my own father swam many times in the waters around these Keys islands looking for springs."

I set a piece of fish down in front of each cat while Juan was talking. As hungry as those cats had been acting, not a one would touch the fish. They just stared at Juan and stole little glances at the fish there in front of them.

"My father never found the spring of youth in his life, but he did become a rich man working as a diver. He worked for a man who found the wreck of a treasure ship from our homeland."

Juan snapped his fingers once and all the little pieces of fish disappeared instantly.

I asked if maybe they had asked some of the Indians about the fountain. Juan Ponce stiffened at the mention of Indians.

"There have been many rumors from the Indians for my predecessors. Once a small Indian boy told my father that a clue to the Fountain was in the mother lode treasure. But we Ponces have never trusted the Indians, not since Ponce the First was killed by a poisoned arrow."

The smiling young woman showed up with a double armload of boxes and bags for Juan to carry. She got a good grip on his arm and started in telling Juan Ponce about all the things she'd bought while dragging the sighing juggler down the street. I swear one of those cats winked at me before it ran off behind them.

* * *

The next couple of days I checked up and down Charterboat Row looking for gainful employment, but it just wasn't happening. Key West is a great place to be, but it's a lot better place to be if you got some money coming in somehow.

I found a quiet spot along the water to sit in the evenings, where I could think about things and inspect my hand. I definitely wasn't dreaming being broke in the Keys, and I was getting a little worried.

Chapter 22

Room 325-C
Big Pelican Nice Lucky Motel

Jeremy woke mid-morning, face down, wedged between the bed and wall. He wasn't sure where he was at first. He was only sure he had a roaring headache and his bladder was nearing critical mass.

The effort it took to crawl into the bathroom woke him up enough to vaguely remember hugging the commode at some point during the night. The discovery of his obvious lack of accuracy during the previous evening's projectile vomiting prompted yet another round of retching.

After a quick shower, Jeremy came out of the splattered bathroom and took off his soaked clothes. He laid the shirt and shorts on the chair next to the window air conditioner to dry, wadded up his underwear and lone remaining sock, and threw them in the bathroom. He toweled off and took stock of his belongings. Still had his wallet and gold card, but the pocket mirror was missing.

He was so happy to find his boots in the room, he gave them a quick wipe before crawling into the bed for a nap.

After a few of hours of oblivious sleep and several extra-strength aspirin, Jeremy put on his almost-dry clothes, and got a complimentary cup of burned coffee from the lobby under the watchful eye of André.

"Yo, Chief! You might want to have somebody check the lock on my room. I had a hell of a time getting the key to work!"

André's sincere apologies and assurances of prompt action satisfied Jeremy, who then helped himself to some stale complimentary candy and some freshly expired Disney coupons. He marched out scorching his tongue on the coffee while André sighed and went back to playing Hearts on the office computer.

Back in the room he checked out the booklet of information on treasure he had bought from the big, surly bouncer at the club. It was a weathered book with no cover, but it had a lot of information about treasure ships that had sunk around the Keys. Jeremy was feeling pretty good about having gotten the price down to only a hundred dollars until he saw the last page that said, "Compliments of Keys Real Treasure Museum — Key West, Florida."

Jeremy's stomach growled, signaling it had recovered sufficiently to begin accepting small, easily digestible donations. Since it was already afternoon, he decided to grab a cheeseburger on his way to the Pink Snapper.

* * *

Thus began a routine for Jeremy that was to have little deviation for the next few days. The one slight difference being that the next thing he bought from Butch was a treasure map for seventy-five dollars, which was the same one the gift shops on Duval Street sold for five dollars.

Chapter 23

Capt. Tony's Has Some News for Taco Bob

"… one of my more memorable nights."

I was sitting in Capt. Tony's bar one evening, nursing a beer after a hard day of fishing for grunts and looking for work. It was another warm evening, and the place was filling up. Word has it that Capt. Tony's is one of the places where ol' Hemingway used to hang out.

Anyway, I'm sitting at the bar with a crossword that had me stumped. I gave it a rest, and started thinking about the last emergency twenty I got folded up in the corner of my wallet. Across that smoky old barroom I noticed this fella wearing an eyepatch sitting at a table by himself. I'm looking at this fella and thinking he's somehow familiar. About then he turns and looks over at me with his one good eye, and I realize it's ol' One-Eyed Pete, one of my former employees from the possum ranch.

This is some kinda great news, so I go over there and we're all shaking hands and bear hugging and happy and shit. We then proceeded to spend some prime time catching up and drinking up. I had completely forgot him telling me once about his sister moving to Key West. She was there with her husband and kids, so he'd been staying with them when he first hit town.

"Got myself lucky and got me a killer job, Taco. Sis told me about this writer fella, Mr. Shirt, got a boat and a house here in Key West, needed somebody to run the boat and keep an eye on things while he was in New York, which is most of the time.

"Mr. Shirt give me the job taking care of his 36-foot Bartram, which he don't hardly go out on much on account he tends to get a mite seasick sometimes. Spends most of his time when he's in town over at his house writing books and hanging around naked in his pool in back."

This was sounding like a fine set-up for Pete, and I was proud for him.

"So Taco, what you been doing with yourself here in the land of the conch?"

I finished off my beer and took my turn.

"Before I got to Key West, I had a few encounters with the Dalton Gang. I'm sure you remember those two knuckleheads, the ones got caught back in Texas after forty-nine armed robberies, nearly all of them filmed by surveillance cameras."

"Sure, I remember. You were on the jury. They're the ones robbed a bank once and forgot the money. They still play that video on TV once in a while."

"Shoot, I was the dang jury foreman! Those mean-ass varmints got it in their heads I'm the one caused them to get sent up. Their uncle was the one gave 'em the five years when we found 'em guilty after a forty-five second deliberation."

"It's been five years already?"

"Not exactly. Those rocket scientists broke out of prison four days before they were due to get released."

We both did some slow head shaking and beer-sipping over that.

"But since I got here, I been mostly learning to catch some fine-eating kind of fish called a grunt that goes quite well with grits, and due to current cash-flow concerns, I been kind of camping out in my truck."

Pete ordered up a couple more beers, leaned back in his chair, and got him a good grin started up.

"Man living on grits and grunts, and sleeping in his truck, might be proud to know my sister done heard from Hop the other day. Said if Taco Bob come through town to have him call out to Texas. Turns out your membership in the Possum Ranchers Association had a nice insurance policy with it. Said he's got a check for ten thousand for you now and plenty more coming later."

Needless to say, this was some kind of good news, and it set off another round of handshaking, grinning, and bear hugging.

"Mr. Shirt I work for said he wanted me to keep an eye out for somebody to house-sit his place here in town while he's gone, since I been staying on the boat most of the time. We can give the man a call in the morning if you're interested in the job, maybe get a-hold of Hop and get you some cash wired in too."

So I'm leaning back in my chair, squeezing Key Lime juice in a cold Corona beer, and letting a grin have its way with my face. Some money coming in, a job with a place to stay, and Pete running a big-time fishing boat seemed to all of a sudden have everything covered for me. Well, almost everything. Pete seen the crossword I had on the table and picked it up.

"Let me take a look here. You know, I can't hardly see a crossword puzzle these days without it reminding me of possum ranching."

I showed him where I was stuck, a five-letter word for change that starts with a "w." Pete always had a knack for crosswords, so I let him scratch his head on that while I went back to my beer and pleasant thoughts.

"It ain't 'woman'; that don't quite work."

The song playing on the jukebox ended just as Pete had it.

"I got it! It's 'witch'!"

I looked over to the door just then, and who walks in the bar but this good-looking young gal with buzz-cut hair who works at the bakery where I've been getting my morning coffee. She came straight over, gave us a big smile, and sat right down there at our table.

Turns out she knows Pete because she's staying with another woman at the place next door to Mr. Shirt's house. So ol' Pete introduced me to Mary Ann.

"I know this guy! He lives in his truck parked behind the bakery and gets coffee there in the morning!"

Pete thinks this is real funny for some reason and starts in laughing. While I was busy blushing, I noticed the gal's toenails were painted black with the big toes sporting little white skulls and crossbones.

"How long you been living here in Key West, Mary Ann?"

She gave me a strange look with some mighty fine big eyes.

"Not long. How long you been living in that old truck of yours?"

She didn't seem to want to talk about herself, so I told her some about leaving Texas, staying in Panama City and working my way on down to Key West. I was about to order another round of beers and launch into a few exciting, and mostly true, anecdotes about life as a possum rancher when she made the time-out sign.

"I don't suppose you'd like to come by my place and use the shower, would you? I'm pretty sure I have some beer in the fridge."

I looked into those big, laughing, brown eyes, and you could have knocked me over with a feather. I was kind of embarrassed and all, but she was just a-grinning at that, and well, I hadn't had a good wash with soap and hot water in a while. I looked down at my hands for a quick finger count to make sure all this wasn't going to turn out to be some dream. When I came up with five, I checked again and started up grinning myself.

* * *

I ain't going to bore nobody with the details, but it was one of my more memorable nights. It'd been a while since I was with a good-loving woman like Mary Ann, and when I woke up the next morning in her bed, I was having a much better outlook on things.

Chapter 24

A Much Better Outlook
for Taco Bob

"Life is sweet!"

I found Pete after Mary Ann ran off to work, and we got some cash wired in from Hop for pocket money while that first insurance check worked its way through the mail down to the Keys. I offered to send Hop some money later if he needed it, but he said he was doing fine and had himself a good job already doing accounting for some Internet company.

We called Mr. Shirt up in New York and struck an even better deal than I'd hoped with the housesitting. Turned out I'd get a little salary just for keeping an eye on things while I was staying there.

So I was off straight away, celebrating my new prosperity with a used bicycle for touring the island in style. It seemed like the sky was bluer, the breeze sweeter, and the people even friendlier with things going my way. I figured I would have the money to buy a nice flats boat with enough left over to live on for at least a few months before I had to worry about finding a job.

I spent the rest of the morning riding around Key West just grinning at life, eating an ice cream cone, and waving to the tourists wandering around Old Town looking for the perfect T-shirt or the best deal on a scooter rental.

There were parts of the island I hadn't seen yet, so I let my new bike take me along the narrow streets of some old neighborhoods that'd been baking in the tropical sun for a lotta years. As rough as the tropical climate was on buildings, the landscaping sure didn't seem to mind any. Just about every yard had some kind of huge shade trees, palm trees, or exotic flowering plants going on. Some houses had cars out front all decorated up with hand-painted pictures of boats and parrots and sunsets. Other houses there were old men sitting on porches telling stories and keeping an eye on the little kids playing in the street.

In the afternoon I rode about a dozen times by the bakery where Mary Ann was working, grinning ear to ear and waving. Finally, Mary Ann came out and gave me a stern look.

"Taco, you really need to get your silly ass somewhere else so I can get some work done. I can't be looking out the window and laughing at some clown going by on a bicycle every few minutes!"

I gave her my best puppy-dog eyes. That got me a big ol' kiss and she ran back in the bakery, then came out a couple minutes later. Said she was getting off early and got on the bike with me. We rode on back to her place to check if we had remembered to make the bed that morning.

* * *

I got myself set up comfortable in Mr. Shirt's house, next-door to where Mary Ann was staying, and did some looking around at boats for sale the next few days.

Mary Ann and I took to each other like biscuits and butter, and we spent a lot of time just hanging out around town together enjoying each other's company. There were plenty of restaurants around town for us to have some relaxed and unhurried meals, sampling exotic tropical delicacies. Relaxed and unhurried evenings in bed afterwards seemed to just come naturally.

My job housesitting left me with a lot of free time — an important ingredient in your better tropical lifestyles. Mary Ann, on the other hand, kept busy with work. Besides the full-time bakery job, she was working a couple nights a week dancing at a club, one where she'd told me real serious-like she didn't want me coming to visit.

But she had some days off, and one time we caught a ride on a dive boat and did a little snorkeling. Saw all kinds of pretty little multi-colored reef fish and even some big ol' mean-looking barracuda. Mary Ann was a pleasure to be with and interested in everything around her, like she hadn't been getting out much for a long time. I found out the hard way she not only had a great sense of humor but was also a natural-born actress.

One afternoon we stopped by the newly renamed Two Willie's Seashells, where Mary Ann hit it right off with my shell-merchant acquaintances. After a bit, young Willie commenced to wax eloquent on the merits of individual specimens, and Mary Ann was hanging on every word, giving the display of brightly colored shells a good look. The old man and I stepped over into the shade of a big palm.

"Your grandson sounds like he's been paying attention."

"Boy seem to know a lot more about them shells when they a pretty woman around."

He gave me a wink. Mary Ann, wearing her usual skintight shorts, was bending over to check out a lower shelf.

"This lady, she seem like a nice girl for you. Built nice too."

"Yep, I sure been lucky to meet her."

"You tell her you a expert grunt fisherman?"

"Uh, no. That ain't come up in conversation just yet."

"You should tell her, mon! Show her a stringer of nice grunts sometime. Women, they like these kind of things, this I know!"

While I was filing away this important piece of information for future use, Mary Ann turned around holding two pink shells the size of footballs. She held one on each side of her neck and batted her eyelashes.

"What do you think, Taco? Earrings?"

"I would say a mite large, but what do I know?"

She put her nose in the air and turned around to the grinning Willie.

"The man obviously has no fashion sense. I'll take this one my handsome young friend."

I paid for the queen conch over the protests of the eldest Willie, who then offered to demonstrate his musical talents. Both Willies got into it, blowing into the big conchs and before long a pretty good crowd had come up. There was a break in the show and a little applause from the tourists. That's when she got me.

Mary Ann snatched up her conch shell and held it to her chest like it was a long-lost child. As she took a step back from me I thought I saw her give the Willies a little wink, but there was fire in her eyes when she let me have it right there in front of everybody.

"I'm done run off an' leave my husband and three chil-drens and sick momma back in Alabamer, an' come down here with you in your fancy car with your fancy talk, and now you won't even buy me no damn seashell?" She caught me off guard, but I tried to come back.

"But, sugar-dumpling!"

"Don't you be sugar-dumpling me none! You get me down here in that fancy motel with that air condition and color teevee, and get me doing all kinds of things on the bed and then you taking all them pictures! I swear, if I wasn't carrying our love-chile, I'd —"

"There a problem here?"

It had to be the biggest Cuban cop I had ever seen. Man looked like a finalist in a scowling contest.

Mary Ann was holding her own, but her eyes were laughing. Both Willies were looking down and highly involved with straightening up their shells. I thought I heard a snicker get loose from the old man as I came up with my best smile.

"No sir, officer, no problem! Little lady here just got a touch too much sun, makes her a bit excitable sometimes. We'll be going now, get her in the shade for a cool drink. Everything's going to be just fine."

The crowd of tourists parted to let us through, and I had to pull Mary Ann along by the arm while she was giving her audience a last look of total innocence and confusion. Willie couldn't hold it any longer, but the cop didn't seem amused.

"What's so funny, old man?"

We only got about a block away before we had to stop because Mary Ann was laughing so hard she was about to fall off the bicycle.

* * *

I decided that if before long I was going to be fishing the waters of Key West in my own boat, I needed to dress the part. We checked some shops and I got set up with some pants with zip-off legs and the latest in vented shirts with Velcro pockets. I was in style, of sorts, except for the hat. Never could find anything I liked better than the ol' straw hat with the sides rolled up I'd paid a dollar for back in Panama City.

It being Key West, a young woman with buzz-cut blonde hair and a scruffy-looking older guy in fisherman's clothes strolling down the streets arm-in-arm didn't bring much notice. I was finding the place just as laid-back as all those songs said it was.

One day we were walking down Duval Street and my flip-flop broke. It was a goner, so I went native — barefoot as a duck.

"Taco, we better go by your place and get some shoes."

"I'm okay, maybe I'll spring for a new pair of flops later. I want to stop by Margaritaville for a drink first and see if there's anyone wasting away in there."

About ten more steps and I found an old soda can pull-tab the hard way. My normally sympathetic companion rolled her eyes.

"Now you've done it. And don't look at me like that, you know it's your own damn fault."

Mary Ann stopped the bleeding from the cut on my heel with a scarf and we cruised on back home for a blender-full of medicinal beverages and a band-aid.

* * *

By the time the insurance check got to me, I'd located a nice little flats boat that a condo Yankee was selling at a good price. Flats boats look kind of like one of those bass boats I used to have that the tornado tore up so bad. The main difference is most flats boats are white and have a little roof over the motor you can stand on to look for fish and push yourself along with a pole in the shallow water. They're great for sneaking up on fish.

So I bought the boat and headed out exploring all that gorgeous water around Key West most days. Pete went out with me a few times and we got into catching bonefish and pompano, sharks and barracuda, snapper and grouper, and one time a few grunts that I proudly presented to Mary Ann. Her and I took some trips on the boat checking out the little islands around Key West and found some nice private places for swimming and snorkeling.

I still hadn't come up on what I'd call the Ultimate Fishing Experience, but life was sweet on the little island at the end of the road. It seemed like the good times would never end, and I was going to sleep every night looking forward to the next day.

Chapter 25
Checking on Jeremy

Carol was feeling good. Nothing like a little time on stage in front of adoring fans, even if they were Charlie's fans, to build a girl's confidence. Carol was feeling so good about her performance the first night at the workshop in Germany that she stuck around even after Sara made a miraculous recovery. The next night, the new head of the Spider Cult was decked out in her latest designer ensemble by Frederick's of Hollywood, warming up the enthusiastic crowd with some of Charlie's old jokes. She was having such a great time she didn't really want to call Jeremy, but she knew if she didn't stay on his ass, he wouldn't get anything done.

* * *

"Jeremy, you slimy worm, you better have some news for me from the treasure museum."

Jeremy was pacing back and forth next to the bed in his tiny room.

"Shit, Carol! When have I had time to go to some dusty old museum? There's something wrong with the water here; I keep getting food poisoning every night! I'm telling you, Carol, this place is the armpit of the world! I'm lucky to still be alive in this primitive backwater town!"

Jeremy ignored the things on his bed: a Key Lime pie, a basket of conch fritters, a fried grouper sandwich, half a large sausage pizza, an empty champagne bottle, several skin magazines, three new Hawaiian shirts with matching shorts, and a naked, overweight, snoring prostitute. The TV was on the Playboy Channel with the sound turned down. With a cigarette dangling from his lip, he had the phone in one hand and a large frozen drink with a little umbrella in the other.

"Not that you would appreciate it or anything, Carol" — Jeremy took a sip of the Margarita and tried to work the TV remote with his toes — "but I've been cultivating some sources of information with the locals here."

"I'm sure you've got your finger on the pulse of what-ever passes for sleaze down there, Lover-Boy, but you better have some solid leads on the treasure scene when I get there."

Jeremy choked, spitting some of his drink on the bed.

"You're coming here? You won't like it, Carol, trust me! The place is full of sweaty, sunburned tourists drunk on overpriced booze, and everything is covered with seagull shit. The locals are uppity, and there's no high-end shopping for a hundred and fifty miles!"

"Thanks so much for your concern, Jeremy, but I'm sure I'll get by somehow. Meet me at the airport at 6:30 tomor-row evening, and be ready to take me to whoever has my idol."

Jeremy stood with the phone to his ear, listening to the dial tone for several seconds after Carol hung up. He finally decided the best course of action was to quietly grab his stuff and slip out of the room. Jeremy headed for the Pink Snapper for a drink and a serious strategy session.

Chapter 26

Sam

Sam Turbano sat at the end of the bar. He drank coffee while casting a seasoned, judgmental eye over the early shift of losers filtering into the Pink Snapper. He hocked up a wad, spit on the floor, and mumbled something to the bartender, who quickly refilled his coffee cup. No one else even looked at Sam. He was a dried-up old man in a rumpled suit, sitting in a dark, dingy, topless bar in the middle of the afternoon on a bright sunny day.

Sam didn't care about going outside in the brilliant sunlight these days; the light hurt his eyes. He'd spent most of his life out in the sun, diving for treasure and raising hell around Key West. As a young man, Sam had made a reputation for himself in the Keys as a selfish and quarrelsome bastard. The only thing that had changed as he got older was that he got older. He was a mean old cuss.

Sam had always liked money and women. He also liked hiring and firing people, mostly firing. That's why when he found the mother lode treasure years ago, he'd bought the Pink Snapper with part of his money.

Rumor had it that Sam had screwed his partners out of shares of the treasure when they finally hit it big. People said there was even more treasure on that old ship than what had been brought in, and that Sam had it hidden away somewhere. There were threats and lawsuits for years. Sam finally won by simply outliving all his former partners.

Chapter 27

Life at the Snapper

Butch was getting tired of this clown from California in the cowboy boots. He had already scammed the moron for several hundred dollars the last few days. It was easy, really. He simply saw to it that the guy was sitting as close to the stage as possible, then waited until he was out of his head on booze and the sight, sound, and smell of sweaty naked women just out of reach. Then the guy would cough up money for just about anything to do with treasure as long as he didn't have to leave the bar to get it.

It was time to cut him loose though, and Butch figured he might make some points with the old man if he let Sam have him to fuck with. His boss was bad about that. He really liked to mess with anyone he thought he could intimidate. If it wasn't for the fact that Sam treated Butch like shit too, he would almost look up to the old bastard.

* * *

Sam checked his watch. Another five minutes and the first dancer of the day, a Cuban girl named Amee, would be late, again. Sam saw one of his bouncers walking across the bar toward him with a big stupid grin. What was his name? Bubba? Brad?

"Yo, Mr. Sam, how you doing today?"

Beavis? Brian?

"Look, there's this guy over here, been asking about treasure,"

Buck? Bert?

"and I figured, you being such a treasure expert and all."

"Fuck off, Bruce. I got no time for another asshole tourist wants some hot deal on treasure to impress some broad. Get your ass back to work or hit the road, Barney!"

"Uh, it's Butch, Mr. Sam. This guy, he's looking for a particular piece. Some little gold idol that looks like this."

Sam gave his employee a hard look, took the picture, and held it to the light. He stared at it for a few seconds, then took his glasses from his pocket and put them on. When he looked up, he was feeling a little lightheaded.

"Where'd you get this picture from, boy?"

Butch straightened his shoulders a little.

"The little guy with the cowboy boots over there by the stage. Been coming in here the last few days. Says he's got somebody willing to cough up some serious jack for that piece. I told the —"

Sam's hand came up, and Butch got quiet. A young woman ran in the front door and went straight into the back room.

"Tell him to come over here. And tell Amee if she's late again, she's fired."

Chapter 28

The Days of Treasure and Treasure Hunters

Before they found the mother lode, they knew they were close. In about 20 feet of water just inside the reef near Bird Key, a lump sticking up a little higher than the rocks around it turned out to be iron, an ancient iron anchor from a Spanish ship. The next day they found a barnacle-covered cannon, and everyone in the dive crew was pumped.

After years of searching, this was the most promising thing they'd seen. The divers worked longer and harder than ever, but six days later they hadn't found anything else. The men were exhausted and disheartened. Back then Sam Turbano was head man on the treasure team, but he still took a shift in the water every day. The men usually stayed on the big boat for a week or so at a time, diving every day when the weather was good.

Sam had been in the water checking a new area further out, and was turning back to come in when he saw a rock formation he wanted to get a better look at. But it wasn't rock — it was silver bars. A stack of bars almost two feet high, and even more bars spread out over the bottom, sticking out of the sand.

Here Sam's years of practice at being an asshole came in handy. He hid his excitement over the find by going off on one of his screaming rants when he got back to the boat.

"That's it! I want you shitheads to pack it in for a few days before somebody screws up and I got a dead diver on my hands. Go get yourselves some sleep and some pussy in Key West. And try not to get too fucked up, I want to hit it hard again Monday morning."

Sam would stay aboard with the boat's captain and do some work on the equipment.

As soon as his men set off for civilization in one of the skiffs, Sam broke out a bottle of Scotch and had a drink. Old Bart, the captain of the ship, wasn't one to turn down whiskey. Sam left him the bottle, after slipping a couple of barbiturates in it, and grabbed himself some sleep.

When Sam woke up a couple hours later, he found Capt. Bart passed out on the floor of his cabin, snoring loudly. He got his gear loaded in the other skiff and slipped out into the night. It took him almost an hour after he had anchored to find the silver bars. Even with the big underwater flashlight, things looked a lot different swimming in the pitch-black water at night. Sam didn't bother with the silver, he was looking for gold.

And he found it. Coins, necklaces, and figurines, some just lying there, some under decades of silt and ocean crud. His light reflected jewels scattered across the sandy bottom in places, and he spent several hours picking through treasure and going back to the skiff, stopping only to change scuba tanks.

Just before dawn, an exhausted Sam pulled himself into the skiff. He started the motor and did a quick check of his gear and the extra gas he'd put aboard. He didn't see any sign of life on the big boat as he headed north with two full sacks of Spanish treasure.

*   *   *   **

At first there were suspicions about Sam when it was discovered that someone had already disturbed the area around the silver bars. The partners calmed down some though as the treasure kept coming in. Even without what Sam had taken that night, it still turned out to be the biggest treasure find in Florida's history.

Chapter 29

Meet the Man

Areosmith's "Teacher" blasted from the sound system inside the Pink Snapper. The first dancer of the day came out on stage in a skimpy schoolgirl outfit, wearing her hair in pigtails and sporting an oversize pair of horn-rimmed glasses.

Jeremy was transfixed. His palms started sweating as he unconsciously kept checking the wad of one-dollar bills he had in his front pocket for the dancers.

Suddenly, the big, stupid bouncer who had screwed him on the treasure map was in his face. Jeremy couldn't hear what he was saying because of the music, and was trying to look around him at the dark-haired dancer with the incredibly firm-looking tits.

Next thing Jeremy knew, the asshole had a big meaty hand under his arm and was walking him roughly away from the stage, yelling in his ear, "Somebody wants to talk to you."

When they got close to the old man sitting at the end of the bar, the geezer gave a dismissive wave of his hand and the big jerk let go of Jeremy's arm. Jeremy shrugged his shoulders and made a token gesture at straightening his shirt. He turned to give Butch a look, but found himself alone with the old man.

"So what's up, Chief? You got something on your mind, old dude?" Jeremy didn't like the way the guy in the rumpled suit was looking at him.

"Sit down. What do you know about this?"

The old guy set the picture of a little golden idol on the bar in front of Jeremy.

"Hey, that's one of my pictures! You got some information for me?"

In less than two minutes, Jeremy's mind went from Lust Mode to Panic-and-Fear Mode. Now Greed Mode was kicking in. It was making him a little dizzy; he sat down facing Sam.

"This is my bar; I own it. I'm asking the questions. Tell me everything you know about this picture, or I'll have Bruce come back over here and squeeze your little bald head until it pops like a big zit."

Chapter 30
Buried Treasure

Sam ran the skiff with the bags of treasure back up through the Keys and then north into Florida Bay, looking over his shoulder every thirty seconds. He stopped at several of the dozens of little deserted mangrove islands before he found one he liked, not too far from the mainland near Cape Sable.

Having thought of everything except a shovel, Sam used the little Danforth anchor from the skiff to dig a hole and bury his gold. He stopped digging every few minutes to check in all directions to make sure no one was around to see what he was doing. It was a beautiful clear day, and back then there wasn't much boat traffic. Only once did Sam see another small boat way off in the distance.

After making sure he'd left no signs of digging, and even smoothing over his footprints in the sand as he left, Sam made his way back to Key West, still looking over his shoulder every few minutes.

He should have been ecstatic with the treasure he and his partners were about to start bringing in after years of search-

ing, but all he could think about was his two sacks of buried gold. Sam was a nervous wreck thinking about it when he got back to Key West, so he decided to go to the topless bar, have a few drinks, and look at some titties to take his mind off things.

The more he drank, the more it began to dawn on him that he was about to become a very rich man. The more he drank, the better those titties looked. It didn't take too long before Sam and the whiskey decided he could take his pick of any of the women in the bar that night. The one shaking her ass in front of Sam's face right that moment was his first choice.

Sam had a good grip around the dancer's waist and was halfway to the door, when a stocky bartender with a shaved head and a baseball bat got in the way. Despite the naked woman squirming and screaming, Sam was holding his own one-handed against the bartender, who seemed to think he was Roger Maris going for home run number 61. He had just sent Roger back to the bench with a kick to the nuts, when the owner of the bar stepped up and pinch-hit Sam hard across the back of the head with a pool cue.

Sam loved a good fight as much as the next mean bastard back in those days, and he didn't mind fighting dirty either, as long as nobody tried it on him.

The pool cue made a loud crack when it broke over Sam's head. The soon-to-be-former owner of the bar stepped back and looked at the madman holding the frantic dancer like she was a stuffed toy he'd just won at the carnival. He expected the madman to go down. He didn't.

Sam froze and looked at the now still and wide-eyed blond dancer a second, then shook his head sadly. He let loose of the woman, turned, and charged, roaring headfirst at the soon-to-be-leaving-town man holding half a pool cue.

* * *

Within a few days, Sam had recovered from the beating he received that night from the police batons before spending the rest of the night in jail. He would go back out on the big dive boat with his men, find the mother lode, and become rich and locally famous. He bought the bar from a man who would then move to Orlando to get in on the ground floor of the topless bar scene just before Disney hit town. The man eventually became rich himself, but had difficult bowel movements for years due to an incident he did not care to discuss involving a pool cue.

After that night, the blond dancer thought she could never get enough of Sam. But after living with him for a few weeks, she decided she'd definitely had enough, and headed for Orlando herself.

Sam enjoyed the money and even liked the attention from the press at first. He bought a nice house in Key West and settled into being a local celebrity and owner of the only topless club in town. But mostly Sam worried about his two bags of gold buried on the mangrove island in Florida Bay.

Chapter 31

Butch's Job

Butch decided his job wasn't all that bad. Sure the old man was a pain in the ass and never gave him any respect, but it paid good and had some decent bennies. Getting to hit a drunk in the face with some parking lot once in a while was one of them. Another was intimidating the dancers. Though that was only until they found out he was just hired help and not the manager. When Sam found out Butch had been telling people he was the manager, he told him to get his head out of his ass or he could go back to renting jet-skis to tourists for a living again.

But driving the car was a plus. Butch knew he was cool in his wrap-around shades and Hawaiian shirt with the little pink parrots open over his black T-shirt with the picture of Stone Cold, his current favorite wrestler.

Since rolling up the dark-tinted windows in the big black Mercedes would keep people from seeing how cool he was, Butch took the long way to the airport in the old man's car with all the windows down and the air conditioning and sound system cranked to the max. He'd driven the old man around a few times, but this was the first time solo. He bobbed his head to the music and hoped the old fart would let him use the car more often.

Chapter 32
Pirate Jim's and Taco Bob

"Free beer with chowder!"

Some fool in a big black car just about run me over as I was walking across the street to a little place called Pirate Jim's. It ain't a very big or fancy place, so I sat at the bar and ordered up a bowl of their famous by-catch chowder and a beer. I was still a little shook from my close call and the ol' fella sitting next to me asked me what was up.

"A big Mercedes just about took my kneecaps off when I was crossing the road just now. I don't think the fella ever even seen me, had his head down messing with the radio."

The ol' guy had white hair and beard, and reminded me of a scrawny Santa. With his skin the color and texture of shoe leather and the white splotches of bird poop all over the shoulders of his threadbare work shirt, I had him pegged as a local.

"Lotta that going on here these days. Old days, man could get blind drunk, walk all over the island and not get run over but once or twice all night. These days it's hardly safe crossing the street stone sober!"

He punctuated that bit of timely information with a loud belch, which was answered in kind by the green-feathered source of the bird droppings that was perched on his faded old captain's hat. I'd never heard a parrot belch before.

"Had to drink a lot of beer to teach that damn bird to do that." He gave me a big wink. "Name's Fish Daddy, and that's Capt. Tom up top on the poop deck." Upon hearing his name, Capt. Tom let loose another long parrot belch.

I told him my name was Taco Bob, and we did the hand-shaking thing just as my chipped bowl of steaming chowder and warped spoon arrived. I was hungry, as usual, so I got my spoon bent back to where it resembled an eating utensil and dug in. I ordered another bottle of Samuel Adams for my crusty new acquaintance and another draft for myself.

"Yes sir, I would imagine Capt. Tom there's a real crowd-pleaser at some of your better social events around town."

"He shore is. Women like him too, 'specially drunk women!"

The ol' fella thought this was way funny and went to laughing. The beers arrived just in time for him to down half of his to settle the coughing jag that followed his laughing. I was busy polishing off my chowder.

"You ever had any of that chowder you're throwing down before, young fella? Back in the old days, Pirate Jim used to make it up himself, you know, in a big ol' oil drum out back. Couldn't afford shrimp, got all the weird stuff the shrimpers usually threw back, made his chowder with that. Had just a hint of a fuel oil taste first few batches." The wall behind the bar was covered with all kind of pictures; one was a big cartoon drawing of a grinning Pirate Jim stirring a drum of chowder with a boat oar.

"Stuff was so bad he had to give away a free glass of beer with every bowl. Course that was before that boy dressed up like a manatee got famous. Got his start right here, playing guitar and singing for tips and chowder."

I realized I was in the presence of a genuine Key West barstool-historian.

"Sounds like you been coming in here a while then, Fish Daddy."

"Shit. I come in here times when I didn't have much money, which was most of the time. Had me a good thing going for a while though, running pot back in the '70s. When that all went to hell, I worked nights for a while getting lobsters outta traps so them boys wouldn't have to lift so much. Got outta that when one fella got in a lucky shot."

He slipped off his stool and pulled the back of his shorts down to show a big puckered-up scar I could have gone without seeing.

"Worked shrimping for a few years, then got in a all-night card game one time upstairs Sloppy Joe's. Drunk fella used to work as a treasure diver in there thought he was that ol' boy discovered Florida or something. Anyway, it was my lucky night, and by morning I'd won me a pot full of money. The liquor and women was a few weeks of damn good times with half the money, and I'm still living off the rest I put in stocks and bonds. I may be crazy, but I ain't stupid!"

With that he issued forth a heartfelt belch that was again answered in spirit, if not in volume, by Capt. Tom.

I got another round of beers and we got into trading stories for a bit. Since it got to be a habit by then, I was looking at my hand, taking a finger count, and he noticed. The ol' fella had a surprise for me.

"You doing that there for lucid dreaming, Taco?"

I hadn't been mentioning my new hobby to folks much lately since it usually just got me strange looks. I hadn't even mentioned it to Mary Ann, worried she'd think me weird, reading a book by Charlie Spider.

But since he'd asked, I told the man that's exactly what I was doing it for. So in between taking pulls on a beer and giving Capt. Tom sunflower seeds from his pocket, Fish Daddy started in telling me all about lucid dreaming.

"I been waking up in my dreams for years, knowing damn well I was dreaming, before I ever found out some yankees up in one of them fancy universities was calling it lucid dreaming. I read up on it some, that guy Charlie Spider's books and even some of them fancy university books them yankees wrote."

The waitress who seemed so well practiced at ignoring Fish Daddy started wiping down the bar within easy listening range.

"Most times, it seems so damn real it's hard to believe it's a dream. Never have been able to get used to that."

He took out a folding knife the size of a small machete and started working on the toenails of one of his bare feet while he went on.

"Now, there's some folks can go into lucid dreams from being awake, but most of us got to hope we got the sense to pick up on some kind of cue in the dream, like you and counting your fingers. I myself usually just look at my dick."

The waitress rolled her eyes and worked her way further down the bar. He gave me a wink and went on.

"From what I read, and from my own personal experience, there ain't much you can accomplish from those kind of dreams though, except maybe curing some people of nightmares. Of course, you can fly around in your dreams, like superman, and all kinds of neat shit like that."

He put the knife back in his pocket and leaned in close like he was going to whisper a secret. He gave a little look over his shoulder to make sure the waitress was noticing.

"Of course the best thing is the sex."

He was whispering till the last word, which he gave plenty of emphasis and volume. He then continued loud enough for most of the room to hear.

"Damnedest sex you could ever imagine too! See something you like in your dream, just go right on over there and have sex with it! Long as you can stay lucid, it's as good as the real thing! Shit, some of those women in the books say it's better than anything they ever had awake!"

Everyone in the place was listening in at that point, and the waitress found a spot closer up the bar that needed more wiping. Even the bird seemed to be paying attention.

"Safe too, don't have to worry about picking up no diseases or nothing. There ain't no pissed off husbands or boyfriends to worry about, don't have to buy 'em no sit-down dinner, and they don't get all mad if you don't call the next day either!"

Fish Daddy went off into a good laughing and coughing jag after that. Everybody else just shook their head and went back to their own business. I ordered another beer for the first lucid dreamer I'd met, then headed out the door keeping a wary eye out for big, black cars.

Chapter 33

Carol and Flying

Carol hated to fly, but she was getting used to it. Of course, flying without an airplane would be a rush, like Charlie had talked about, but she was terrified of heights and would probably completely freak if she ever did it. But then she never saw Charlie do it either. In fact, he never did do much of anything except talk and party. Well, there was the sex. Damn, but old Charlie had been great in the sack.

Carol held that thought and leaned back in her seat. She was starting to get a wet spot in her French-cut designer panties when the plane's captain came on the intercom and announced they were making their approach to Key West.

* * *

As soon as she got off the plane and into the terminal, Carol started looking for Jeremy. As expected, the little worm was nowhere to be seen, just a bunch of odd-looking people, most of them dressed far too casual for Carol's liking. She was about to check the most likely place for him to be, the airport bar, when someone behind her said, "Hey, are you Carol Derrière?"

Carol turned, took a step back, and checked out the big, dark-haired guy with the prominent nose. Actually, he didn't look too bad, in a big dumb-lug sort of way. The bright green shorts and the extra hairy legs were a bit much though.

* * *

Butch had gotten to the incoming flights area just as the passengers were coming off the plane. Back at the bar, Jeremy had been a little hesitant to tell the old man about Carol and the Chacmool Idols after the mention of the head-squeezing thing. But when Sam offered him free drinks for the rest of the night, Jeremy gladly told everything he knew.

So Butch had a pretty good description to go on. That had to be her: tall, with short, dark hair, nice body, skintight designer jeans, and some kind of lacy top that looked like something out of a lingerie catalog. She didn't look too bad, in a snob-class, slutty way. Maybe could stand to lose a few pounds.

* * *

"Who wants to know?" Carol thought this guy might be someone from one of the seminars who'd recognized her. After all, she was a star in her own right these days. Well, kind of.

"Look, lady, Mr. Sam sent me to pick you up. He's a big man in this town. Him and Jeremy —"

"Jeremy? Where's Jeremy?"

"He's with Mr. Sam down at the club. I'm supposed to take you there."

Carol didn't like it.

"Why didn't Jeremy come himself?"

"Uh, him and Mr. Sam were talking, about treasure, and they asked me to give you a lift. My name's Butch. I'm, uh, the manager of the club."

Butch was smiling, obviously trying to look sincere. She weighed her options, then had the big goon help her with the luggage.

* * *

The early evening heat and humidity was an unwelcome surprise for Carol when they walked out of the terminal into the parking lot. It wasn't really that much different than Southern California, except the humidity made you sweat like a pig if you did anything more strenuous than breathe.

Carol rode in back, as she decided her current status as leader of the Spider Cult called for. The bozo reluctantly put the windows up after Carol mentioned it three times.

"Shit! Now I've got something in my eye!" Carol figured what the hell, worth a try. "I told you to put the damn window up. Now I've got some dust or something in my eye and I can't get it out! Pull over somewhere and help me out here. This is your fault!"

* * *

Butch wondered if he reached around and popped her a good one in the eye, that might do it, but he turned off onto a side street and found a place to pull over. The old man would probably get pissed if he brought her in from the airport with a shiner.

"Jeez, it feels like something big. Look in my eye, maybe you can see what it is."

Butch put the car in park and turned around to look into the bitch's eye. The left eye.

*   *   *

Carol was feeling pretty good about herself. Maybe she was getting better at this Black Eye stuff after all. It sure worked on Tall, Dark, and Stupid here.

This old guy Sam Turbano sounded like the person she needed to see all right. Carol had gotten all the information she needed about treasure and Jeremy out of Butchy Boy in just a few minutes. She wondered what else she could get out of him while he was so willing.

Though she was a woman of impeccable taste, Carol was still a woman. A woman with needs. Reaching over the seat to check out what kind of equipment Butch was packing, she noticed a little Indian kid had his face pressed against one of the car's dark-tinted windows, trying to look in. Carol didn't like that at all.

She tapped Butch on top of the head with her knuckles to snap him out of it, then sat back in her seat and sighed.

"Take me to your leader, earthling. I can't wait to meet your boss."

Carol gave the kid the finger as Butch put the car in gear.

Chapter 34
Treasure Check

Sam couldn't stop thinking about his bags of gold. He knew they were safe. There was no way anyone would ever find them, but thinking about that one boat he'd seen way off in the distance was enough to keep him eaten up with worry.

After a couple of weeks he couldn't stand it any longer and made a run out across Florida Bay in his brand new skiff early one morning. After making damn sure no one was within sight of the island, Sam beached the skiff, ran up, and started digging.

He found a place in the middle of the island where he could stand up and see all around to check for other boats. Spreading a blanket, he emptied out both bags.

It was a beautiful clear day. Sam sat down on the ground and spent several hours cleaning and admiring his treasure. It was quite impressive. There were some quality pieces, mostly bowls and cups, but a few heavy necklaces with medallions. Several nice idols and figurines, some jeweled daggers, coins, and a few things Sam wasn't sure what they were. But it was mostly gold, over a hundred pounds worth. Nice little tax-free bonus, he figured.

Sam put the gold into a metal chest he'd brought along, and hauled everything back to his boat so he could go find a better place to hide his treasure. He filled the hole back in with a shovel and was covering over his footprints when he saw a lone footprint off to the side of where he'd been walking. He froze. A big rainstorm had come though the Keys just a few days before, so this was a fresh print. It wasn't Sam's boot that made the print either; a medium-sized bare foot had made this one.

Sam looked around but didn't see any more footprints, just that one. This was not good. He thought seriously about taking the gold back to Key West with him. He already had enough trouble with his treasure partners now as it was. If someone saw him with any extra gold pieces, he'd be in deep shit. He needed to let this stuff sit for a while, maybe even a few years.

He spent the rest of the day looking for another hiding place and finally got the chest buried back up in a tangle of mangrove roots on another island.

It was almost dark when Sam finished, and the mosquitoes were getting bad. He was just bringing the skiff up on a plane when he thought he saw another boat off in the distance. A commercial crab boat it looked like. Sam swore and kept on going; it was dark enough that chances were, the crabber didn't even see him, much less know where he was coming from.

Chapter 35
Carol and Sam

It was a typical early summer storm coming ashore in Key West. The sky to the west was black, so the daily edition of Tropical Sunset was a complete bust. The crowd at Mallory Square quickly thinned out and people on the streets of Old Town hurried to get where they were going. The wind rattled the palm trees and thunder boomed. Cats frightened by the thunder made frantic last-minute dashes in the alleys as the first big raindrops hit the pavement.

Coming back from the airport, Butch pulled the big car around the back of the Pink Snapper and popped an orange tabby making a break for a dumpster. He gave himself a thumbs-up. Carol almost hurled. They ran in a side door of the club just as the sky opened up and it started pouring.

Once inside, Carol started following Butch toward the back, but then stopped. Butch turned.

"What?"

"Just give me a second here, Big Fella."

She looked over at the stage where a slim woman with long red hair and nice boobs was slowly gyrating to the too-loud music. Sure enough, there was a bald head she recognized sitting at a table close to the stage. Carol started toward Jeremy.

"Hold on, Princess, he ain't going anywhere. Mr. Sam said to take you straight in to see him."

Carol looked at Butch's big paw on her arm and gave him her best sneer. He let go and she gestured with her hand.

"Lead on, Handsome."

She looked over at Jeremy and saw he was holding a folded dollar bill up toward the redhead.

* * *

The office in back was a little less seedy-looking than the rest of the place. The room was brightly lit and the walls were adorned with framed pictures of a younger version of the old man now sitting behind the desk. There were some photos of him with people, but there were many more of him posing with his treasure along with laminated newspaper clippings with headlines announcing the discovery of the mother lode.

The current edition of Sam wore a suit that looked a couple of sizes too big. He leaned forward in his chair a little. He looked old, wrinkled, and pissed-off, but his eyes were locked on Carol.

"Have a seat."

The old man waved the back of his hand at Butch.

"Blow!"

The big guy started to say something, but changed his mind and left the room, closing the door behind him. Carol took a seat in front of the desk and held her Gucci purse on her lap. She gave the look she was getting across the desk right back, and then some. The old geezer flashed the briefest smile and seemed to relax a little.

"Okay, little lady, you probably know who I am by now, and I got a pretty good idea of what you're about from your boy Jerome. He says you want to buy the idol he's got a picture of. First thing I want to know is where you got that picture of the Golden Chacmool."

Chapter 36

Treasure Trouble

Several weeks went by until Sam was able to get back to his gold. The salvage of the mother lode off Key West was going full steam. Now that they had cash flow there were more divers at the site, which drew plenty of attention from the press. Sam did some research on Spanish artifacts and saw some pictures of things he had in his treasure chest. One was a curious reclining figure, which was identified as a Chacmool.

* * *

Sam hadn't seen a soul for miles. As soon as he pulled the boat up to the mangrove island where his treasure was stashed he felt something was wrong. He grabbed the shovel and made his way through the tangle of mangrove.

It had been gone for a while. Sam could see where there had been rain at least once since someone had taken his chest of gold and left him with an open, smelly hole in the black mud. Sam Turbano hadn't cried since he was a little kid, but he sat down right there and made little moaning sounds for several minutes.

His grief eventually turned to anger. He looked around and found a footprint just like the one he'd seen before. Someone obviously had seen him on the island. Probably saw him on the first island too, but hadn't been able to find it there. The only boat he'd seen that day had been the crab boat way off in the distance. Had to be it.

By the time he got back to Key West, Sam had decided on a plan of action.

* * *

A few days later, Sam's inquiries paid off. Someone told him a bartender from Marathon had been around trying to sell a gold necklace. Sam found the bartender, who told him an old crabber had sold it to him for a hundred dollars a couple of days earlier. He said the crabber's name was Mikey, and he had a little shack out on one of the islands in Florida bay. He came in to the fishhouse to sell his crabs a couple times a week. Typical crabber, always went to one of the bars on Marathon and got drunk whenever he got a little money in his pocket.

For five hundred dollars Sam got the necklace, the general location where Mikey had his shack, and an understanding with the bartender that they had never had that conversation.

* * *

In the bottom of the boat were a couple of barracuda that Sam had caught while he was waiting for Mikey to wake up.

Mikey had come in late from the bar, staggered up to his tarpaper shack on the island, and taken a good long piss out-

side the door. That taken care of, he pushed the door open
and passed out into bed. Sam had been waiting inside in the
dark, where the mosquitoes weren't quite as bad. He tied the
old crabber's hands behind his back and tied his legs at the
knees. He dragged the unconscious little man out to the skiff
and dropped him inside.

A couple of hours later, the boat was drifting with the current as Sam cut the barracuda into large chunks and dropped
them into a bucket. The sun was starting to come up under
some low clouds when Sam stood up, turned Mikey over on
his back, and pissed in his face.

"Time to wake up, Sleepy Head!" Sam had never been so
mad at another human being.

Mikey groaned and opened his eyes. He tried to sit, then
realized he was tied up and in trouble.

"What's going on? What the fuck's going on here?"

Sam sat back down and dropped a chunk of 'cuda in the
clear blue water. He was just barely able to control his rage,
but tried to keep his voice calm.

"I need you to tell me what you did with my treasure. No
bullshit old man. Just tell me where it is."

Sam dropped two more bloody hunks of fish over the side.

The old crabber was coming awake fast now and was trying to size up the situation. He was scared, and his eyes
showed it.

"Shit, Mister! Look, you got the wrong guy, I don't know
anything about no gold!"

Sam shook his head and sighed. He grabbed Mikey by the
hair and stuck his head over the side so he could see the big
bull sharks that were swimming just a few feet from the boat
now. Sam let loose of the old man's hair, and Mikey fell back
and hit the back of his head hard on the floor of the boat.

Sam dumped the rest of the barracuda over the side and grabbed a leg.

The old crabber was so terrified he could hardly talk.

"I, I m-moved it!"

"Tell me where!" Sam held a bare foot over the side of the boat, his arms shaking with rage. Mikey lost control of his bladder and a dark stain moved over his pants.

"Jesus Christ, Mister! I'll tell you! I hid it at the house where —"

A seven-foot bull shark stuck its head out of the water and clamped razor-sharp teeth into Mikey's foot a split second before the crabber started screaming and thrashing around in the bottom of the boat. Sam held on to the leg with both hands, but the shark shook its head and was gone with most of the old man's foot. Mikey was screaming his head off, kicking Sam with what was left of his feet, getting blood all over him and everything else. Sam got his belt off and pulled it tight around the bloody leg so Mikey wouldn't bleed to death.

Mikey stopped screaming and struggling. He'd had a heart attack and was dead.

* * *

Sam carefully checked the shack and the area around it that day, trying not to make it look like someone had disturbed anything. People forgot about the missing crabber after a few weeks. Sam came back and took Mikey's shack completely apart, then dug under and around where it had been. He used a metal detector and searched every square inch of the island, even the area around the island at low tide.

He kept track of any treasure that came on the open market over the years, but there was never a trace of anything from the missing chest until he saw Jeremy's picture of the Golden Chacmool.

Chapter 37

Gretta

Gretta just about shit when she saw Carol. She was well into her first set of the evening and down to her silver g-string and long gloves when the head of the Spider Cult came in the side door with Butch. Carol was dressed like a Frederick's of Hollywood model, which was different from the usual sexless baggy clothes that Charlie had made his girls wear. But then, Gretta was sporting a different look as well, at least at the moment.

* * *

Gretta was twenty-seven and had lived with Charlie since she was nineteen. She'd been on the run from an abusive boyfriend and an even worse family situation, when she went with a friend to one of his early lectures. Charlie had taken her in and patiently taught her about sorcery and sex. Gretta had seen a lot of women come and go in the group since then. He'd been great at first, but soon tired of her, as he was always looking for someone new. She stuck it out with Charlie, though, even when he became a major control freak as his little harem grew.

When Charlie died in such a horrible way, Gretta bolted. She just wanted to get away from the Spider Cult and everything to do with it. She didn't have a passport or much money, so she looked at a map and determined the place farthest from LA in the US with decent weather. She rode buses until her money ran out, then hitchhiked the rest of the way to Key West.

* * *

After the initial shock of seeing Carol, Gretta tried to keep her long red wig over her face until her former fellow Witchette went into the back with Butch. She'd cut her already short hair down to almost nothing and had even been using a different name, her real name, since she left California.

Carol had looked her way and started coming over once, but luckily Butch had stopped her. Gretta had no idea how she'd been tracked, and it was creeping her out, bad. To top it all off, the little bald guy in the boots that always sat up front was suddenly looking a lot like a guy she'd seen Charlie talking to a couple of times.

Gretta wasn't going to hang around to see how this played out either. Jose was leaving in the morning to take his wife and kid to Disneyworld for a few days. She could probably catch a ride with them, maybe get a job in Orlando. She was going to hate to leave Key West, but she wouldn't miss this sleazy job. She would miss the people she had gotten to know at the bakery, and she was especially going to miss Taco Bob.

Chapter 38

Idol Minds

Neither Carol nor Sam was happy with the way their little meeting was going.

Sam had decided that this woman with her chest about to explode out of a black lacy top didn't have the golden idol from his long-lost treasure. Sam knew she was the head of some kind of cult out in California, so there was no telling what she wanted with another Chacmool or where she had gotten the first one, the one in the picture. She might even have a whole collection of the things for all he knew.

The woman said she'd inherited it from her uncle, who had bought it years ago in Mexico. Before he died, he'd told her there was another one that had gone down in a Spanish treasure ship around Florida.

She said it had been her uncle's dying wish that she find the other Chacmool, and she was prepared to pay better than the market price for it. When Sam asked her why her uncle would have wanted her to have two Chacmools, she said, in a matter-of-fact way like it was really obvious, "So I would have a pair, of course."

This broad didn't have his idol or she wouldn't be here trying to buy it. Sam didn't trust her any farther than he could throw her, and if it came to that, he'd have Buster do it for him.

* * *

Carol was pretty sure the old fart didn't have her Chacmool, but he was sure interested in it. He must have at least seen it before. She wondered what he would do if she pulled out one of the Chacmools she had in her purse. No way Carol trusted this guy enough to do that though.

She had offered to pay the big bucks for the piece, but that didn't even get a rise out of the geezer. Carol sure hated to spend the money; she'd hoped to get the last Chacmool on the cheap. But she figured once she had all three, she could control anyone she wanted, that is, after she learned how to do this lucid dreaming stuff. Then whenever she wanted to do some shopping, she'd just have some billionaire slip her a few million.

But things weren't going anywhere fast here, so Carol decided to make a gesture.

"Look, Mr. Turbano. I want the idol, and you seem to know something about it. Why don't we work together on this? I might have resources that could help find the piece. If we find it, I would at least pay you a finder's fee."

* * *

Sam thought he could probably find out more of what Carol knew by slapping her around some, but the way women were these days, she'd probably get all uppity and not want to cooperate. He didn't trust this fancy bitch, but he didn't have any better ideas. He decided to throw her some bait and see where she ran with it.

"There was a crabber up the road at Marathon years ago named Mikey Smith. Rumor has it he sold a gold necklace in a bar up there, a necklace that might have been from a treasure find. He disappeared and nobody has heard from him since."

Carol seemed to be giving that some thought.

"Did he have a wife, or girlfriend, or any relatives around here?"

It was Sam's turn to do some thinking. He'd been careful not to do much asking around after Mikey had fed the sharks that day. A few months later he found out that the old crabber might have had some relative, a young girl, but she'd left town and the fisherman who told Sam about it didn't remember her name. He hadn't thought about that in years.

"I think there was a girl, a cousin or niece that lived around here, but I don't know her name or whatever happened to her."

Sam was lost in thought when Carol got impatient on him all of a sudden.

"That's it? A missing crabber with maybe a cousin who might have had a gold necklace? Is that all you've got?"

Sam saw red. He glared at the cult bitch and she started backing down.

"Okay! That's something! Don't blow a tube here! I'll see what I can do with that and get back to you." She got up and headed for the door. Sam cleared his throat.

"There is one other thing. He might have hidden something around a house, but not the house where he lived."

* * *

Carol left Sam's office and found Jeremy holding up a dollar bill to another dancer. The loud music made conversation difficult, so she decided to forgo formal greetings and just grabbed the little worm by the ear and headed for the door. Once outside, Carol decided that the best short-term solution to everything was to kick Jeremy's ass.

* * *

She figured it was just poor judgment, or poor timing, maybe both. A police car cruising by the Pink Snapper mistook Carol, an obvious woman of class, for a perp while she was strangling Jeremy with her bare hands. It took some explaining, but Jeremy saved himself even worse problems in the future by explaining to the redneck cops that Carol was his boss and it was all right.

"Really, Officer, she does this all the time! It's like, part of my job description!" Jeremy came up with a marginally earnest smile.

The cops finally left, and Carol calmly strolled through the evening tourists down Duval Street with Jeremy so she could find a more secluded spot to finish strangling the little slacker.

Some sort of primeval survival instinct must have triggered inside Jeremy. He was suddenly interested, trying to be helpful; so Carol told him about Mikey Smith the crabber, the necklace, and the young girl. Telling him made her realize just how little she had so far. Maybe check around town and see if there was anyone else who knew the treasure scene. Do some checking somehow on the old crabber.

She decided to deal with Jeremy later. Right now she just wanted a good meal and a long, relaxing bath. Carol got a taxi and told Jeremy to get her bags sent over to her suite at the Hilton.

As the taxi dodged roving bands of gaudily dressed tourists, she wondered what you had to do to get laid in this town.

Chapter 39

Daltons

A rusty old pick-up truck. Two ex-cons pulled up to a traffic light on Duval Street. The driver was a small man. He looked over at his partner.

"Let's go over it again. What are you going to say if anyone asks what we're doing in Key West?"

The big man stopped eating out of a grease-stained paper bag, his face showed deep concentration.

"I don't say nothing! If anybody asks me anything, I ... I don't say a damn thing!" He gave a proud smile and took another bite out of a burrito.

"Yeah, Lenny, that's real good. Maybe next you could remember not to talk with your mouth full."

George looked at the big bear of a man next to him dribbling food down the front of his shirt.

"I don't know how you can eat those things. God knows what that old guy with the shower cap puts in 'em."

The light changed and they crept along slowly with traffic. The big man sucked down the last of his food and licked his fingers. He narrowed his eyes, looked around cautiously, and went to a conspiratory whisper.

"George, are we gonna steal furniture and rob people again, like we did before we went to prison?"

The little man gave him a fierce look. "I TOLD you not to say that! We did our time, at least most of it, but we're free men now. We're going to make a new start!" George pushed his hair back with his fingers and smoothed it out with the palm of his hand; the big man copied his movements exactly.

"Okay, so things didn't go too good in Miami. Taco Bob wasn't there, and we had a few tough breaks; but I've got a new plan. As soon as we kill Taco Bob, we'll try out this sweet new scheme I been working on. In fact, maybe we'll even give her a try right away."

This seemed to make the little man happy, which made the big man happy. Lenny wadded up the empty food bag and dropped it out the window, one hand going into his pocket. George noticed.

"What have you got in that pocket?"

The big man looked pained. He slowly pulled his hand out, but kept it closed.

"It ain't but a little stone crab, George! I was just petting it! I ain't hurting nothing. It's already dead!"

The little man rolled his eyes and gave his partner a disgusted look.

"It's gonna start to stink!"

He held his hand out as he stopped at a light in front of a T-shirt shop.

"Give it here, Lenny, right now!"

The big man looked like he was about to burst into tears but handed over the crab. As soon as it touched George's hand, he flung it out the window toward the crowded sidewalk.

"Jesus H. Fucking Christ! It's already starting to smell! I don't know why I put up with you sometimes, Lenny!"

The big man wanted to say something to calm his partner in crime. "Is it because I can carry furniture out of houses so good?"

"I told you to forget about that! I got a plan, a good plan this time. I got the idea while I was working in the prison library. There's a lot of writers living in Key West, right?"

Chapter 40
Mama Rosa

Mama Rosa had moved to Key West twenty years earlier with her husband Georgio. Georgio was semi-retired and sold a little real estate. It wasn't a great life, the cost of living was high, and there never seemed to be quite enough money at the end of the month. It got too hot in the summer, and every winter the island got a little more crowded with tourists.

But they were comfortable, and they were happy to be away from the winters of Dayton. When Georgio had passed on suddenly three years ago, Mama Rosa started telling fortunes a few nights a week in the back room of a T-shirt shop. She'd read a book once on fortune telling, and since Key West was the place where people were known to try just about anything once, she'd decided to give it a shot. It still wasn't a great life, but at least she wasn't in Dayton.

* * *

The little bald guy who just left had been different from the usual tourist who would slap down twenty bucks to be told there was romance/sex/money/adventure just around the next corner. This guy had some story about treasure and was looking for a crabber who had disappeared years ago. Said he'd been standing out front, thinking about the crabber and looking at the Fortune Teller sign, when a crab hit him in the back of the head. So he came in for a reading.

She told him he'd meet a beautiful woman who would fulfill his deepest desires. He said he already knew that, but she wasn't all that beautiful and she better fulfill his deepest desires for what he was paying her. What he really wanted was for the fortune teller to use her psychic powers to find this crabber guy.

So Mama Rosa told him it would be expensive, and he went for it. She got the details and a deposit and figured she'd give her nephew, the private detective in Miami, a call in the morning.

Chapter 41

Saying Goodbye to Taco Bob

"And I was having such a damn good time too!"

I wasn't always an aspiring amateur gourmet chef, but since watching a few cooking shows on TV, I'd been trying out a few new things.

Mary Ann was off working at the club, so I was deep-frying myself some Bahamian mango-grunt loaf for dinner when Pete come by to tell me he got a new job and was leaving town.

"This fella from North Carolina I was talking to down at the marina a couple weeks ago called this morning and made me a hell of a offer. We'd talked a bit about me working for him when he was here, but I hadn't give it much thought since.

"Man calls this morning, says his boat captain quit sudden-like on him and he needs me up there right away for a big fishing tournament coming up. I checked the man out with some folks here. The guy's got a good reputation and

158

two first-class boats up there. It sounds like a helluva deal, TB. I'm packed and flying out first thing in the morning."

I was sorry to hear Pete was leaving, but I was proud for him to be getting the chance to make some good money for a change.

The grunt loaf turned out crispy with a palatable bouquet but a little dry, so we decided to have a drink, especially since it looked to be the last we'd be seeing each other for a while. So it was off to Capt. Tony's for a few laughs, the Green Parrot for the ambience, Schooner's for the music, and Sloppy Joe's for tradition. After the bars closed we shared a bottle of Jack down at the beach, standing knee-deep in the water and singing old possum-rancher songs in the moonlight. We got a cab to the airport before dawn, and just like that, ol' Pete was off on his way to a new life in North Carolina.

I got back to the house just as the sun was coming up. I was feeling a little down and just wanted to get me some sleep and get on with my own life. I got up to the front door, and it was already open a little. Sure enough somebody had gone through the place, tore it up real good, and stole a bunch of stuff.

I went next door, woke Mary Ann up, and called the police. Then I called Mr. Shirt in New York. Mr. Shirt was none to happy to hear the news, especially since Pete had just quit on him the day before. I seen it coming. Sure enough he asked me where I was while someone was tearing up his place. So I told him, and he fired me.

So I was sitting there in the kitchen with Mary Ann, waiting on the police to show, and I was starting to get a real bad headache. Mary Ann had been acting kind of strange since I got there, and then I found out why.

"I hate to have to tell you this, but something's come up, and I have to finish packing because I'm leaving town in a little while."

Having been up all night drinking, I wasn't at my most alert. At first I thought she was trying out another one of her jokes, but her eyes told me it was the truth.

"It doesn't have anything to do with you, and no, you can't come along. I don't really want to talk about it. It's something I have to do by myself, and I'm afraid I really do have to leave right away."

About then the police showed up next door. So with Mary Ann telling me she really liked me and was going to miss me, I went on over there in a bit of a daze. The big Cuban cop I'd seen before was there, and I told him who I was and that I had been out with a friend all night and that friend was gone to North Carolina now.

They put the cuffs on me, for my own protection, and stuck me in the back of a patrol car. By then there was all kinds of cops rooting around in the house, and plenty of locals to come over and gawk at me sitting there in the back of the police car. An old Chevy pulled up next-door with some big guy driving and some other people in it. Mary Ann came out with a couple suitcases, got in, and the car left. I was really getting a bad headache.

Some new cops showed up and one came over, gave me a real mean cop look, and asked me the same questions the other cops had already asked. After every cop and most of the locals in Key West had checked out the situation to their satisfaction, they took me on down to the police station so they could ask me the same questions a few more times.

I ended up sitting in a little room with a bare table, two chairs, and a phone on the wall. There were two cops in the room too, Sergeant Goodwin sitting in the other chair across the desk, and Sergeant Badowski yelling into the phone.

The cop across from me smiled pleasantly and told me to just call him Larry. The other cop finished up his phone conversation by telling someone that if it came to that, try to make it look like an accident. He slammed the phone down and stared pacing. Larry pulled out a pack of smokes.

"Cigarette?"

"No, thanks."

"Coffee?"

"Uh, no, I'm good."

Badowski was still pacing, looking down at the floor and shooting glances at me.

"Soda, candy, gum?"

"No, thanks." I tried a smile of my own. "But I could sure use a couple hours sleep."

Badowski slammed both hands down on the table in front of me and got in my face.

"Where's your partner? Is he still in Miami? How long have you been in Key West? Don't try to shit me here, we know you're linked to that liquor store robbery by the Interstate, the reststop car-jacking, and a string of attempted robberies in Miami. You may as well save yourself and everyone else a lot of time and come clean with us now!"

I let that hang a beat or two before I came back.

"The two people come closest to a partner I got both just left town this morning, and I ain't ever been to Miami, much less done no car-jacking or liquor store robbing. And I'm sure y'all checked my record already. My only two encounters with the law before today was a few days in a Texas county jail for improper toxic waste disposal, and three days of jury duty that ended up netting me fifteen dollars a day and a death threat."

This wasn't the hoped-for response, obviously, since Larry stopped smiling, and the other cop started yelling into the phone at someone about making room in the pit for another one.

But after a couple more hours of my answering the same questions, the police finally came to grips with the stark reality that I was innocent of breaking into the house where I lived, tearing it up, and stealing stuff. They turned me loose in the afternoon after giving me more mean cop looks and telling me not to leave town.

So I immediately set about getting my stuff together so I could leave town. Things were going bad fast in Key West. It seemed there were only two things that could be worse, and I wanted to get away for a few days before they showed up.

Got my camping stuff and plenty of food together, parked my old truck over at Pete's sister's place, and lit out in my flats boat.

I headed northeast out of Key West. I had overheard some fellas in the bar talking once about some old abandoned house up near the Chatham River on the mainland above Cape Sable. It sounded as good as anything, so I checked my charts and started the long run along the Keys and across Florida Bay.

Chapter 42

Ten Thousand Islands and
One Stormy Night for Taco Bob

"… and a cast of millions, all skeeters!"

It was a beautiful clear day with flat seas when I left Key West, but by the time I was getting up on the mainland near Cape Sable, the weather was turning ugly. There was a real mean-looking storm coming from the west, and I was getting my ass beat from the big waves it was kicking up. I was still a ways from the Chatham River, and it was almost dark. Being low on options out there in the middle of nowhere, I decided to run up one of the closer creeks and ride out the storm.

I was just about up to the big wall of mangrove trees that passes for land along there when the rain stopped messing around and got really bad. It was raining so hard, it was stinging my eyes and I couldn't see where I was going anymore. I slowed down and waves started coming over the side of my boat, then I heard a real loud roaring noise, and suddenly I was in the water.

I got my head up out of the water, but the storm was so bad and it was so dark, I couldn't see anything. I was having a hard time with the waves and was getting tired out fast since I hadn't had any sleep the night before. I started to panic.

Somehow I had the sense to check for bottom, and sure enough I could just barely touch my toes down between the big waves. I figured out which way the land was, and started kind of swimming and hopping over that way.

The worst part of the storm finally passed, and I got into some shallower water. By the time I got to the mangroves, I was completely exhausted. I pulled myself through the mud up on a knot of mangrove roots to rest and was greeted by the worst swarm of mosquitoes I'd ever seen. I went back in the water and just lay there in the shallows with only my face sticking out of the water, trying to get away from the skeeters. Somehow I still had my hat, so I put that over my face to try to keep the bugs off and passed out for a while. I had a real bad night and didn't get much sleep because as the tide went out, I'd have to move to deeper water to get away from the skeeters.

* * *

At first light the bugs seemed to get even worse for a while, but I got up out of the mud anyway and looked around to see where I was. All I could see was water to the west and mangroves and black mud to the east. My face was all swollen from skeeter bites, and before long I was flat worn out walking up that creek in the waist-deep water, looking for my boat.

But I finally found her, jammed up high and dry in the mangroves. It must have been a waterspout had come out of the storm to put my boat up in there like that. She didn't seem to be torn up too bad and was right side up at least. Most of my stuff was gone, but I did find a few things, including a raincoat. I crawled in the boat and covered myself with the raincoat and tried to get a little sleep.

In spite of the heat and the bugs, I did manage to sleep some. Then I shook myself out and took stock of my situation. I found a couple fishing poles, my tackle box, a frying pan, and a wet bag of grits, but most all my supplies and the big cooler with my drinks and water jug was gone. The boat was stuck bad, but I decided I might be able to get it back in the water at high tide if I could cut enough of the mangrove away from it. There wasn't nothing else around neither, just mangrove trees fifty feet high as far as you could see. Not hardly a bush or a blade of grass anywhere, just mangrove and black mud.

The boat was quite a ways up the creek, and I didn't know if it would do me any good to wade back out to the open water to try to signal a passing boat. That whole section of the state is part of the Everglades National Park, and there ain't nobody living around there for miles. I knew there wouldn't be much boat traffic coming along anyway, especially that far down into the park.

I got the anchor out of the boat, set it on the mangrove roots, and made a driftwood fire on it because there wasn't any actual land, just a solid tangle of mangrove roots over the mud. I managed to cook up some grits to eat, but I was sure thirsty. I waited until the tide started going out good before drinking any of the creek water, but it was still kinda salty.

I found my Swiss Army knife in my tackle box and used the little saw to cut the mangrove holding my boat, but it was slow going. Then it started getting dark and the bugs got bad again.

I curled up in the boat and covered myself with the raincoat, but by the next morning the bugs were getting to me and I was feeling kind of sick. I wasn't hungry anymore, so I just went to working on them mangroves again with my little saw; but I got tired quick and had to go lay down again in the boat.

By afternoon I was feeling even worse and decided if I didn't get some help, I was going to be in serious trouble. I figured my only shot was to go back out the creek and hope someone would come by in a boat close enough I could signal to 'em. I crawled out of the boat holding onto my raincoat and eased on into the water, but I got dizzy and was about to pass out, so I leaned back against the mangrove roots.

I realized I must have lost track of time somehow because it was almost dark, and I was getting the shakes, when I saw what looked like a little man standing on a log up the creek not far from me. I got up and started walking in the knee-deep creek over that way to get a better look, but I tripped on something under the water and fell.

The only other thing I remember from that night was laying on my back, looking at the stars moving along through the tops of the mangrove trees and my head hurting real bad. I couldn't move because it felt like my hands and feet were tied up, and something was tied across my mouth. Then I must have passed out again.

Chapter 43

Dreams for Taco Bob

*"I slept for a long time and
had the damnedest dreams!"*

*I was floating. I was floating on my back in the cool water
of the creek and watching the tree leaves shimmer in the
warm peaceful sunlight above me. My body felt strong and
aware. I heard laughter in the distance and slowly turned
and swam to the shore so gently that I hardly made a ripple
in the water. I saw a big alligator sunning herself on the bank
just a few feet away, but I had known she was there and
slipped out of the water so quietly that she did not even open
her eyes.*

*There were other boys walking through the dense woods,
and I joined them. We moved without leaving a trace. We
didn't even brush against a branch, and we walked so softly
that we left no footprint, no sign of our passing. We moved so
quietly even the birds did not notice us as they chattered and
called out their songs in the trees above us. We came into the*

village with berries and roots and helped our parents and sisters prepare the meal.

Our days were spent exploring the woods and swamps and creeks. I learned the songs of the birds in the trees, ran with the deer and swam with the fishes and turtles of the water.

On the full moon, we rode in the giant trees that our parents had made into water vessels and made our way to the great water to gather shellfish for our feast. We swam in the salty waters but did not fear the shark fish because we swam with our brothers the dolphin, who would warn us of danger and protect us.

One day the Elders called me to them. I sat on the ground before the old ones, and they told me of wondrous things. Then I knew that two of the Elders were the earth mothers, and they sang in my ears. The third Elder was the sun. He placed his eyes on mine and I went to a place of many beautiful visions and songs. But they were too many for my young mind and they became too strong and powerful. A fierce guardian challenged me, but I was too weak and his presence burned inside my head.

I held my hands over my eyes until the pain passed, then looked for the guardian but saw something was wrong with my hands. One hand had only four fingers. Something started coming out from deep inside me and then there was only pain. I cried out.

Chapter 44

It's a Small World for Taco Bob

"The best soup I ever had, bar none!"

I woke up in a cold sweat with a terrible headache. I was lying on a mat with a plastic cover, looking across a small room at an ancient cast-iron stove over by a screen door. The only light came from the doorway and one window. I slowly sat up.

The only other things in the room I could see were a table, a chair, and a pile of rags in a corner near where I was lying. For some reason I really liked that place. After I sat there and thought about it, I realized I liked that place so much because there weren't any mosquitoes.

I laid back down, hoping the hammering in my head would ease up some, and noticed some kind of dried roots or something hanging from the ceiling rafters. Then I noticed the pile of rags had eyes and was watching me.

That shook me, so I tried to sit up again, but I was real weak and dizzy, and I eased back down. About then I real-

169

ized I was naked with a little blanket over me, and there was a strange humming noise in the room.

The pile of rags was a little old man, and he was humming a song I seemed to recognize. I asked him where I was but he just kept on humming that song, and a little while later I went back to sleep.

* * *

The next time I woke up, there was more light coming in the window and door, and I could see better. The little old man was sitting there still, and I got the impression that he opened his eyes the same time I did. He stood up and stretched, and I got a good look at him. He was just a little fella, maybe had some Indian blood in him, and he was really old.

You know how people look when they get to be a hundred? Well, this fella looked like he had seen a hundred a long time ago. Folks have told me before that I looked a little weathered, but I looked like a new-born babe compared to this fella. This was one leathery-looking old dude with a major case of the wrinkles, and he didn't seem to have a hair on his head either. His clothes was a kind of dirt color, but his little eyes shone when he looked at me.

He made for the door and was gone before I could ask him where I was, or who he was. I was bad thirsty, so I took a long drink from the water bottle I found next to my mat before going back to sleep.

* * *

The smell of food was a pleasant thought; then I remembered where I was and opened my eyes. It was getting dark again, but I was feeling better, so I sat up and seen there was a little fire in the stove that was throwing some light into the room. There was a pot of food on top of the stove, and I was all of a sudden real hungry. The little old man came inside and sat down on the floor in front of me, and started in humming again.

I asked who he was and he stopped humming. He looked me up and down real slow, then spoke in a real quiet voice.

"My name is Henry Small, but you can call me Mr. Small."

"Pleased to meet you Mr. Small. I don't suppose you could tell me just where it is I am, could you?"

"You are here in my house, up one of the creeks that goes into the Lost Man's River."

The old man talked real slow like he wasn't used to talking. His voice was so quiet I had to really concentrate to hear what it was he was saying.

"You don't need to worry about your white boat; it will be fine where it is for now. The sickness is leaving you, but you still need to rest."

Mr. Small got to his feet, and I noticed he seemed mighty limber for a man his age.

"I've been watching out for you the last few days, but it's time for you to start taking care of yourself. There's some soup on the stove; if you're hungry, you can help yourself."

And with that he walked out the door.

I was still a mite weak. I didn't know if I was strong enough to stand up and walk across the room to the stove, but I sure knew I was hungry. So I crawled on over to the stove on my hands and knees.

I got myself set up with some soup, sat there on the floor, and had at it. About halfway through the bowl of soup I realized I needed to go to the toilet in the worst way.

I got to my feet and stumbled out the screen door. I took two steps in the dark and was in the water. It was such a shock, I stood up real quick in the waist-deep water. In no time about a million skeeters descended on my naked body. I eased on back down in the water, finished up what I had come out there for, then went on back in the little cabin and ate my fill of that fine soup.

*   *   *

I spent the next couple of days mostly sleeping, eating a little soup, and getting my strength back. Mr. Small told me since I was feeling good enough to be taking a late night swim, I might be feeling good enough to wash up my stinking clothes. He told me where my clothes and an old piece of soap was, so I give 'em a good washing outside in a bucket of rainwater. Mr. Small brought in some gnarly-looking carrots and taters and onions that looked like something he must have grown in a garden someplace.

There was a stack of old paperback books behind the stove. The old man tore off a couple pages from one of the books, put a match to 'em, and got some firewood going in the stove.

He took a couple of the tuber-looking things down from the rafters and had me cut everything up for another soup while he went out and quick-like caught a little snapper fish for the pot.

I still was a little weak, so I went and sat down on my mat while the soup cooked. The old man usually stayed outside, but this time he sat down on the floor in the same spot where I had first seen him.

"I sure do appreciate you helping me out here, Mr. Small, and letting me stay in your place and all."

The old man just sat there and looked at me with them intense little eyes of his.

"I'm feeling better now, so if you could maybe give me a ride back over to my boat, I'll see about getting her unstuck and be on my way."

Mr. Small didn't seem to be much of a talker, so I went on, "My name is Taco Bob, and I was headed over to a place I aimed to camp out for a while called the Old Watson Place. Maybe you heard of it?"

Mr. Small leaned over a little and started making a muffled coughing noise. I thought maybe he was having some kind of a fit, but then he came up with a big ol' toothless grin and I realized he was laughing. Not understanding what he was laughing for, but not wanting to be missing out on any fun, I started laughing a little too.

The old feller settled down, but was still sporting a grin. His voice was so quiet I had to lean forward to hear.

"I'm afraid you missed out on staying at the Old Watson Place by a few decades, young man. The old house was blown away by a big hurricane a few years after the Park people took over this part of the state. It was the last place left after they took out all the old squatter shacks the fishermen lived in along the coast. What they couldn't burn, they carried off. Other than a few channel markers out in the mouths of the rivers, there's not much sign of man left along this whole area."

I reckon that much talking at once was a bit much for the old man, cause he didn't say anything after that.

"So I take it, then, you don't have much in the way of neighbors."

"Not in the last 30 years or so."

Mr. Small worked him up another gummer smile.

"Plays hell with the dating too."

Then he got serious looking again.

"You were very sick. The spirits came for you once, but they didn't take you. You need to rest and become strong again. You are worried about your white boat, but it is safe, no harm will come to it."

He started getting that grin going again.

"Besides, you have already reached your goal. When the great storm destroyed the house of Watson the Outlaw, I carried the lumber I found from the old place back here and built this cabin you're sitting in now."

Chapter 45
Miami PI

Tommy Arenas was a busy man, so it was several days before he got to the little job that had come in from his crazy aunt down in Key West.

Before he started doing PI work, he'd spent several years as a bounty hunter, running down low-life bail-jumpers. Tommy eventually decided he'd had enough of dealing on a far too personal level with the floor sweepings of society. The final straw was a contract to bring back a career wife beater who'd cut town after his parents put their house trailer up for his bond.

Tommy found the asshole across the state in Naples, where he'd followed the wife to her sister's place. That night, Tommy waited outside the house by the guy's car. When he finally staggered out, Tommy knocked him to the ground and cuffed him.

He put the guy in the back of his car, then turned around and caught a tire iron across the mouth courtesy of the drunken wife, screaming, "Let him go! He's my man and I still love him!"

These days Tommy was trying to do more surveillance and research work for lawyers and insurance companies and less of the in-your-face stuff for the bail bondsmen. It was mostly boring work, but the pay wasn't bad and he hadn't needed any more expensive dental work lately.

He got on his computer and accessed a couple of government sites he wasn't supposed to have access to. In 30 minutes he had a name and address for his aunt.

Chapter 46
Carol in Paradise

Days of dragging Jeremy around with her to the treasure museums and running down dead-end leads on treasure hunters had not improved Carol's mood. It didn't help for Jeremy to keep telling her he had a line on the crabber Sam had told her about, and that he expected to have some news for her any day now.

Of course the little piece of walking crud wouldn't tell her where he was supposed to be getting this information, and knowing Jeremy, he probably was looking in a crystal ball or something equally ridiculous anyway.

Carol cut Jeremy loose one afternoon, went back to her suite, and had a nap. Then she went out to a bar and met some guy named André, who told her he was the manager of the motel with the most rooms in Key West. She acted impressed that he was in charge of the biggest motel on the island and tried not to seem confused when told that it wasn't actually the biggest motel, but it did have the most rooms.

She liked André's good looks and big hands, and invited him over to check out her suite. They did a thorough mattress check until three o'clock in the morning, when a sated Carol told him it was checkout time and to make sure to lock the door on his way out.

*   *   *

Carol had just invented a new chocolate that was not only incredibly delicious, but actually helped you lose weight, when Jeremy's pounding on the door awakened her at nine o'clock that morning. Carol was not amused.

She finally got tired of Jeremy's muffled pleadings and locked herself in the bathroom for a leisurely bath. While soaking, she again reviewed the list of things she planned to do once she had the power of the Chacmools. Amongst the debaucheries involving exotic men, stunning jewelry, fast cars, breathtaking homes, and great piles of cash, she left room for the slow and agonizingly painful death of a certain persistent, door-pounding little vermin.

After carefully dressing in a tasteful bustier and Versace jeans ensemble, Carol opened the door to find Jeremy sitting in the hallway holding an open skin magazine in one hand and the shoe he'd been using on her door in the other.

"Oh, I thought I heard someone at the door." Carol slammed the door and retired to her bed. She hadn't locked it though, and Jeremy burst in.

"Shit, Carol! Where have you been? I tried to find you last night, but you weren't here!"

Carol looked up from examining her nails and yawned. "So?"

"So I got the goods on the crabber's niece. I got a name and an address for you!"

Carol sprang from the bed and grabbed the little man by the ear.

"Give it up!"

Jeremy let out a screech.

"Ack, that shit hurts! Let go, Carol!"

She turned loose of his ear, but stood her ground and narrowed her eyes, starting a low growl.

"Hey, I'm helping you out here! I just want to make sure you realize the trouble I went through to get you this important piece of information."

Carol growled louder and showed some teeth.

"And I want to make sure you are willing to compensate accordingly." Jeremy took a step backwards.

"I want you to teach me the Black Eye thing."

"No way. You know the deal, give it up or you're blowing bubbles in the toilet bowl."

Jeremy got a real hurt look on his face and gave her the sad eyes treatment.

"Aw, come on, Carol, quit being such a hardass. I figured you'd be happy."

Carol was still feeling a little glow from the night before, so she relented, for once.

"Okay, give and I'll cut you some slack. But no Black Eye until I get the idol."

Jeremy thought about it a second.

"Deal. I got it all written down here. She's living on a boat in a marina at some place called Sanibel Island."

* * *

The next day Carol flew out of Key West International Airport in a small 20-seat Air Keys commercial plane to Fort Myers. She looked out the window of the half-filled plane to the east and saw nothing but little dark green islands and miles more of green beyond that. She thought it was strange there weren't any cities; maybe that was the Everglades swamp place she had heard about. Carol read a magazine.

* * *

It was a short drive over to Sanibel Island from the airport, and Carol pulled her rental car into the marina parking lot by early afternoon. She found the office and was told the person she was looking for was living on a boat just past the marine research place. As Carol walked by the old wooden building on pilings out over the water, she noticed a couple of older guys sitting on the porch, drinking beer and seriously checking out her stuff.

Carol found the boat, a houseboat called the *Oar House*, stepped aboard, and knocked on the door. A tired-looking woman with graying hair and middle-age spread opened the door. Carol could hear Jerry Springer on the television. She didn't waste any time getting the woman back inside and having her check out the eye with the black contact lens.

An hour later, Carol left the houseboat knowing far more than she wanted about this woman's relationship with her Uncle Mikey before he disappeared two days before her fifteenth birthday. The woman remembered seeing a gold necklace and had been told there was plenty more where that came from. Carol also found out about an old abandoned house where Mikey would sometimes stay when he was working his illegal crab traps up along the coast in the Everglades National Park.

Chapter 47

Mr. Small, the Swamp, and Taco Bob

"Window screens have got to be one of mankind's all-time better ideas!"

The next few days I ate a bunch of Mr. Small's soup and tried to learn a little about my host and his life in the Everglades. Once, after finishing off a batch of particularly good soup, I was reclined on my sleeping mat, savoring a crossword I'd found in one of the weathered paperback books he used for starting fires. The old hermit came inside, and I found out he was in one of his rare talking moods. I asked him about Key West, and it turns out he'd lived there for a while before moving to the swamp.

"How long ago was that, you living in Key West?"

"Many winters. Some men had built a railroad from the mainland through the islands the last time I was there. I couldn't see any good coming of that, so I moved to the swamp. I wonder sometimes if Key West has changed much since then."

I was thinking SUVs, discount airlines, tour buses, and cruise ships the size of small cities, disgorging hundreds of tourists at a time onto the streets of Key West. Bargain-starved tourists with cellphone cameras, walkmans, and email, filling the sidewalks, shops, and bars, making purchases with gold cards.

"Yeah, I reckon you could say it's changed a bit since the railroad come in."

I was curious about the ol' fella staying in the swamp so many years alone, living off the land. But he said there were other people living out there at one time, mostly pretty tough folks from what I gathered.

"I hated to see all my friends leave when the government took this land, but the way things were going, if the Park hadn't come, there wouldn't be much wildlife left by now.

"The first white settlers shot hell out of the birds for the plumes that were popular then for ladies' hats. They nearly wiped out some species of birds. Fish, turtles, deer, gators all got hit hard back in those early days. Some of the old crackers still came in after the Park people took over and poached gators for the hides."

The old man talked quiet all the time, so whenever he'd pause, all I could hear was the skeeters buzzing outside.

"There was no school for the young ones back in the early days. The children learned hunting and fishing as soon as they were old enough to work a trap or a net. People were living in little shacks with tarpaper walls and palm thatch roofs. Most of the early settlers didn't even have screens on the windows, and had to burn smudge pots to keep the bugs from carrying them off."

I felt like I'd had some recent personal life experience at what that must have been like.

"There used to be Indians living out here too, but most of them moved further inland to the big reservations. It was a free but hard life for the people in those days. There was always plenty of fish for eating and selling though, and some even managed to grow some vegetables and fruit to sell in Key West.

"The Park people grandfathered-in those of us who had been here the longest. That was a long time ago. I doubt there's anyone left these days could find me out here if they wanted to."

I knew what he meant, too. His old cabin had been there so long the mangroves had grown up and around and over it so much, it looked like part of the swamp. You could be fifty feet away, looking right at the little shack, and not see it.

He told me there was a place back up inland a ways, where he had a little vegetable garden and some fruit trees going on himself. Said he'd show me sometime if I wanted.

"When people lived along here, some thought there was treasure. They said the pirate Jose Gaspar and others had treasure hidden along the Ten Thousand Islands because it was the wildest area and the last place anyone would look."

He had a funny gleam in his eye, but he didn't say any more, so I was about to ask him if anyone ever found any old pirate treasure, when he stood up and started spinning around with his arms straight out. I'd seen him doing that before out on the little front porch of the cabin, but this was the first time he'd done it inside, right in front of me. It was kind of weird to see this ancient ol' fella spinning around like some kind of whirling dervish. He stopped after a bit and started doing some kind of stretching exercises.

"Uh, excuse me for asking, Mr. Small, but what in blazes is all that spinning about?"

He was really into the stretching thing and sat down on the floor and did some more before he answered.

"It is for the body, to keep it young. My body was always telling me what it needed, but it took me a long time to learn how to listen." He give me a big wink before answering the question I hadn't asked.

"I looked for treasure like the others at one time, maybe I looked harder than anyone. But I don't look for buried treasure anymore; these days, I'm looking for the Fountain of Youth."

This was some news. I sat back and ran that around while he lay down on the floor and started arching his back up and down.

"I met a fella in Key West, said he was looking for the same thing, Mr. Small. Said he was a descendent of ol' Ponce de Leon, actually. Kinda strange sort, but a hell of a nice guy."

The old man stopped what he was doing and locked onto me with those intense little eyes over that.

"Did he say where he was looking?"

I had to think about that a minute.

"Seems like he said something once about bogs and swamps. Man could juggle cats like nobody's business too."

Mr. Small was giving all that some serious thought.

"Swamps and bogs, he said?"

While the old man was working that over, the realization come over me that we were ourselves currently sitting in the biggest swamp in the state of Florida.

"I think your friend is right. In fact, I think the Fountain is close. Sometimes now, I see it in my dreams."

Which seemed to be all the man had to say on the matter, because he hopped up on his feet and was out the door before I could say anything else.

* * *

I finally got to feeling more like my usual ornery self, and Mr. Small told me it was time to go get my boat out of the mangroves. We got in his little boat, a hollowed-out log canoe like the Indians used to have, and slowly worked our way down the creek. It actually wasn't much of a creek up by where the cabin was at, more like a slow-moving shallow lake, full of trees.

It wasn't much of a boat either. With me sitting in it, the sides weren't but a couple inches above the water. I figured that must have been why I remembered being tied up when he first found me, so I wouldn't go wiggling around and flood the boat. Mr. Small stood in the back and poled us slowly along through the little creeks that mostly all looked the same to me.

My boat was still there all right. A big heron was sitting on it and took off as we came up. I really needed a chainsaw, a winch, and a big helper, but settled for a rusty ax, some poles, and a little helper. It took me a couple of hours of chopping in the heat of the day before we got to try using a couple of mangrove poles to scoot the boat back in the water. For such a little old man, Mr. Small was sure strong. We had timed the high tide just about right and had her floated again by late afternoon. I checked the motor, and she turned over but didn't start. I didn't press the issue because I didn't want to run down the battery.

I asked Mr. Small if I could stay with him again that night, and he said of course, I was welcome to stay as long as I wanted. I thanked him and let him lead the way back to his cabin. Those two boats were about as different as could be, but they were both built for poling, so we slowly poled our way back up in the swamp.

* * *

I decided to take Mr. Small up on his offer and spent a few more days hanging out with him and the critters of the swamp. Since I was pretty well back up to speed, he put me to work mending the roof of his cabin and helping him with the garden. I kept on sleeping on the mat inside, since the old man insisted, and I did sleep awful good there for some reason. He didn't ever lie down in the cabin himself; he would sit there in that same spot in the corner and just kind of stop moving for a few hours sometimes. He spent most nights outside though, so I figured he must have another place to sleep.

* * *

I cleaned up my boat, and thankfully, got the engine running all right. Checked it out from one end to the other and did an inventory of what I had. I found my toolkit all in one piece, and since I still had my pocketknife, I give Mr. Small the little fold-out knife and pliers tool I had in there. He gave that thing a real good going-over, pulling out all the little tools in there, and got his weird laugh thing going again and thanked me. It made me feel good to be able to give the man something he might be able to use, since he'd helped me out so much.

Mr. Small showed me how he did his fishing. It wasn't much different than what some of the big birds did that stood along the edge of the creeks. It mostly involved staying real damn still in a spot where the fish was likely to be and throwing a spear. I watched him do it and I figured I could do that; it looked easy. So of course, it was a lot harder to hold perfectly still than it looked. The skeeters weren't as bad in the daytime, but they were still bad, and that sure didn't help. The bugs didn't seem to bother the old man all that much. When I asked him about it, he said the skeeters got tired of him a long time ago.

The more I was around Mr. Small, the more I realized he always seemed to know what was going on in the swamp all around us, even in places before we got to them. We were easing on over to the garden one time, and he stopped poling and listened.

"I hope that big gator doesn't walk where we put in those tomato plants."

Sure enough, when we got there a little while later there was a big old bull gator swimming away from the high ground where the garden was. I gave the man a look.

"Now how did you know that gator was up here when we were still a long ways off?"

He waited to answer until we had pulled his little boat up on shore. The old hermit had me sit down there with him, where fresh gator tracks went straight toward the rows of little tomato plants, before turning off toward the water.

"There are always circles of energy in the world. Every movement, no matter how small gives off an energy that affects everything around it. Something as big as this lazy old gator here gives off signals that are spread by all the plants and animals around. Just like you might not hear the tree fall in the distance, but you would hear the bird call out that was frightened by the noise the tree made."

I give that some thinking, and was about to ask him again just how he knew about that gator, when he gave a little smile and a wink.

"It's just something I picked up by being out here in this wilderness for so long by myself."

That seemed to be the end of that line of discussion, so I started telling Mr. Small about the real vivid fever dream I'd had when I was so sick. I could still feel the sensation of being very young and moving through the woods without leaving a trace or making a sound. But before I got too far into the telling, and before I could tell him about lucid dreams and seeing my hand just before I woke up, he raised his hand to stop me.

We sat there in the sun with just the sounds of the swamp. Looking down at his hands, Mr. Small started talking even more slow and careful than usual. I had to lean in to hear what he was saying.

"I have had that same dream for several weeks now. All the years I've lived here in the swamp, I have never had dreams like that before."

I didn't know what to say, but I sure thought it was curious we both had the same dream.

"You got any idea what that kind of dream might mean? I been thinking it over, Mr. Small, and I ain't got a clue."

The old man looked up at me with them intense little eyes of his.

"I don't really know either, but I think it has to do with the Fountain of Youth. Sometimes, at the end of the dream, there's a stranger bringing me something, but I never can tell what it is."

We sat there for another minute, and he was looking uncomfortable, like he had something else to say. I was learning some things from Mr. Small, one of them being patience. I waited him out. Finally he cleared his throat.

"There's something else. I saw something moving through the swamp. I could never get close enough to tell for sure, but it looked like a small person poling a canoe. I was following it the day I found you by your boat in the creek."

We sat there for a few more minutes before the old man said it was going to be dark soon, and we'd better be getting some firewood and vegetables together for the evening meal.

Chapter 48

The Watson Place

Carol needed to see Sam. As soon as she got back from Sanibel Island, she told Jeremy to set up a meet with the old bastard. Jeremy, who was still on his best behavior and all full of himself for doing something right, got back to her right away. Sam was in Miami with Butch, but would be back the next afternoon.

As much as Carol didn't like, much less trust, Sam Turbano, she knew he would be her best bet for finding whatever was in this old house the woman at Sanibel had called the Watson Place.

Since Sam was gone, she went to the library and found out what she could about the house.

The fact that it had been blown away years ago by a hurricane was not a good sign for openers. Supposedly, the house had been built on a forty-acre island that was mostly an old shell mound left by the Calusa Indians. This guy Watson was known in the early 1900s for his sugar cane syrup and his habit of knocking off the farm help on payday.

From what Carol could find out, there wasn't much left on the island except an old rusty syrup kettle and a concrete cistern for catching rainwater. She didn't want anything to do with going out to this island where there were probably bugs and no decent restrooms, but she sure didn't trust Sam to go out there without her either.

Carol decided to do what she did best and go shopping for a nice outdoorsy ensemble to wear out to the island. Maybe something in black.

Chapter 49

A Tarpon for Taco Bob

"Hot damn, but that's a fish!"

I was showing Mr. Small the two fishing poles I still had on my boat, and he was checking them out thoroughly. I asked him if he'd like to try one. He said no, but if I wanted to go exercise some fish sometime, he could show me a couple good spots.

The next morning I got a chance to show off my boat to Mr. Small. I followed his directions and poled us on out that maze of little creeks and swamp. When we got close to the coast, the creek we were on widened out some so it looked more like a real river. After carefully looking through my tackle box, Mr. Small handed me a big topwater lure and indicated it was his choice for the morning's fishing. I tied it on my line.

He gazed on up ahead as the boat slowly drifted along with the tide. I stood up in the bow while he was keeping the boat lined up in the current with the paddle.

"On the next corner, the branch that hangs out and almost touches the water. A nice fat snook fish waits there for your lure."

I turned around and stared at the old fella. He had spoken in a clear, sharp, and strong voice. My mouth must have dropped open because he was grinning big and gave me another of those winks before pointing to the place coming up in the river.

I cast, missed the spot by a good ten feet, reeled in fast, and hit it dead center on the second try. The plug lay there on top of that clear black water and I gave it a little bump. BAM! Water flew, and the fight was on!

It took me a few hard-fought minutes, with him pulling line all over the river, to tire that big snook. Mr. Small finally reached down in the water next to the boat, held the fish by the mouth with one hand, and popped the hooks out with the other. As soon as the old man let loose of his mouth, about ten pounds of fish gave a big splash and was gone.

I was grinning ear-to-ear, and Mr. Small was looking kind of proud of himself too. I realized I had the ultimate fishing guide.

We moved on out the mouth of Lost Man's River, and I caught several more nice fish the same way. I was having the best day of fishing I had ever had. Mr. Small asked me if I wanted to go air out a tarpon or two. I'd caught a lot of different kinds of fish while I was in Key West, but I hadn't caught a tarpon.

"Hell yes, I imagine I could use to try out a tarpon, see what all the fuss is about with those bad boys!" So we ate us some lunch we had brought along while catching a few hand-sized pinfish for bait.

I had tried to ask him about his voice while we were fishing, but he said to wait. I tried again. He answered in his new voice after finishing a pear he'd been working on.

"I just wanted you to listen. The way I talked quiet, you had to concentrate to hear every word. Most people, after they hear the first few words a person says, feel they already know what the other is talking about and start thinking about what they're going to say next. So they don't listen carefully and miss a lot."

As usual, he was giving me his full attention. He rarely talked if he was doing anything else at all.

"If you think about it, you'll realize most people's minds are usually running ahead. That's why they don't hear everything that's being said."

I had to admit, it was true for me as well. Before I could get into too much more heavy pondering though, the old man had another surprise for me.

"You aren't the only person I've found troubled in the swamp."

He paused a second like he was making sure I was listening. I was.

"Many winters have passed now. I found an old Indian on a beach once. The buzzards were already circling his body. He had been shot days earlier, and I was surprised he could even be alive."

I reeled in a nice pinfish and dropped it in the livewell. Mr. Small gave me a nod that we had enough bait.

"The old one could not speak he was so weak, and when he did, it was a language I had never heard before. He lay in the cabin for days, fighting death and wanting me to speak to him, tell him stories. He won his battle with death, and learned to speak English."

Mr. Small looked all around like he wanted to make sure no one would overhear.

"The old Indian stayed with me for a summer. He taught me many things about the plants and animals. He taught me how to talk to them and how to listen." He gave that a second to sink in and smiled a mischievous, toothless smile.

"He said he was a brujo, a medicine man. He was the last one to sleep on the mat where you say you sleep so good now."

There was just the littlest shiver went up my spine.

"Before he left, he showed me a power place close by and helped me build a sleeping platform there. The next morning he was gone when I came back to the cabin, and I never saw him again."

* * *

We went on offshore a mile or so to a place where the clear green water dropped off into a deep blue channel, and I seen a couple boats go by way off in the distance. Other than Mr. Small, it was the first sign of other people I'd seen since leaving Key West.

We got the anchor set where we were on the edge of that drop-off, and I got the other rod and reel with heavier line set up with a big hook and a heavy leader with a small float. I put one of the pinfish on there for bait, set him down in the water next to the boat, and stayed ready while Mr. Small stood up on the poling platform real still and slowly looked all up and down that clear, deep channel. It was another beautiful day and there weren't any storms around yet; just enough breeze so it wasn't too hot. I was just noticing that it was the first time in days I'd been outside without skeeters buzzing all around me.

We were both looking along the edge of that deep water when he held up a hand.

"Get ready; they are coming!"

I looked over in the direction he was looking, and I seen a little ripple on the surface of the water and then a big fin come out like a porpoise, but it wasn't a porpoise. Then I saw more fins, and I realized it was a big school of tarpon coming down the channel.

"Cast your little fish up the channel as far as you can!"

I made the throw, then watched the float on the line move around some while the pinfish swam around underneath. The school of tarpon got closer, and I could start to see the dark green backs of individual fish when they'd surface. Mr. Small was holding stock-still, and I don't think I was even breathing as the school of huge fish came closer. The pinfish started getting real frantic and then suddenly jumped clear out of the water. When he went back in, there was an explosion like somebody threw a concrete block in the water as hard as they could. I leaned back into the line hard to set the hook, and the old man was yelling.

"It's the lead fish! You have the lead fish on!"

About then, this silver fish as big as me jumps all the way out of the water, makes a helluva splash, and starts heading west for Mexico in a big hurry.

Mr. Small pulled the anchor, hit the key, and started the outboard up like he'd been doing it all his life. With me standing on the front deck, we were in hot pursuit. The fish had just about stripped all the line off my reel, but in a few minutes, I was gaining some back while the old man motored us along just a little faster than the fish. That big old silver monster jumped again, and Mr. Small said he would guess the fish was easy over one fifty.

About twenty minutes later the fish jumped again but only came about halfway out of the water that time. It was getting tired. I was getting a little tired too, and by the time Mr. Small cut the engine a few minutes later, me and the fish were both a bit winded.

I had to do some heavy rod work to get that big fish up close to the boat, but I finally managed it without breaking the line. Mr. Small leaned over the side, grabbed the fish by the lip, and had his other hand down inside a mouth as big as a bucket, trying to get the hook.

I laid down the rod and reached for my tackle box to get my little one-shot camera. Something hit the bottom of the boat hard enough to make me lose my balance, and I hit the floor. As I was going down, I just seen the soles of Mr. Small's bare feet going over the side of the boat. I pulled myself up as fast as I could and seen a huge hammerhead shark with the struggling tarpon in its mouth swimming away, and Mr. Small splashing around there just a few feet from the boat. I lunged out and grabbed him by the arm and pulled him toward the boat just as another big hammerhead broke off from following the one with the tarpon and come back after the man in the water. I pulled the old man in the boat, and we both fell on the deck just as the big shark missed, making a huge splash right next to the boat.

I got up and checked Mr. Small out. He was holding his hand. There was some blood.

"Mr. Small! Are you all right? Where are you hurt?"

He showed me he'd lost the little finger on his left hand.

"Use this towel and keep pressure on it. We got to get you to the hospital in Key West!"

He shook his head no, calmly sat on the seat in the back, and started in humming. I was in a state. He stopped humming and gave a shrug of his shoulders.

"Don't worry about this, I've survived worse. I always thought it was unusual for a man to have lived so long and not lost even a finger."

I told him again I wanted to take him to the hospital, but he wouldn't hear any of it, just kept on with his humming.

We sat there for a while and I started to calm down. The old man looked out where the sharks had been and stopped humming. A few minutes later he said he was ready to go home.

Chapter 50

Out on the Water

The next afternoon Carol met Sam in his office at the Snapper.

"Okay, I got something for you, partner." Carol checked her nails, making sure the old fart was listening. "I not only found the niece but talked to her. She told me about a house the old crabber used."

This got Sam's attention. He sat up straight and leaned forward in his chair.

"Go on."

Carol held his gaze for a second before continuing.

"We go there together. I want to be around when you find whatever is there."

Sam frowned, then gave her a big smile and held his hands palms-up by his shoulders.

"What, you don't trust me?"

Carol gave him a hard look and a little smile.

"In a word, no. I don't trust you."

Sam lost the smile.

"But you must need me, or else you would have already checked the place out. Quit screwing around. Tell me where the house is and you can tag along. I really don't give a shit."

Carol had figured out there was probably a lot more gold at stake here besides her Chacmool. But she didn't really care about the rest; there was only one thing she wanted. Sam could have whatever else there was, and if he wanted to sell her the idol, that would be a good problem to have because it would mean he had it in his sweaty, wrinkled old hand. She could deal with that.

"We're going to need a boat, there's no road anywhere close. The place is up along the coast on the Chatham River —"

"The old Watson place!" Sam said before Carol could finish.

The old man got a faraway look in his eyes and leaned back in his chair. Carol could see the gears working in the old man's head. He obviously knew about the house. Probably knew hunters and fisherman had used it as a temporary shelter before the storm blew it away. Judging by the look on old Sam's face, this had to be it.

"All these years, I never even thought of that. That must have been where he was coming —"

Sam looked up at Carol and was suddenly all business.

"We'll leave in the morning. I'll need to get some equipment together and see about a boat. And get yourself some decent clothes. This isn't going to be a photo-shoot for Cosmopolitan." Carol gave Sam the finger and stood.

"Call my hotel when you get it figured out, partner."

Carol found Jeremy in his usual place by the stage, and broke the news to him that he was going along in the morning.

* * *

The next morning Jeremy was nowhere to be found. Carol called the dive where he was staying and talked to someone strangely familiar, demanding he find Jeremy immediately.

Sam and Butch already had the rental boat loaded and were getting pissed waiting. Sam had on a pair of square sunglasses that looked way too big for him.

"Look, sweetheart, we got a big day ahead of us here. You coming or not?"

Of all the slimey things Jeremy had done, this was the worst. Carol should have known that his recent behavior of acting mildly responsible wouldn't last.

"Hold on to your hat, Captain Ahab, I'm coming."

Carol was wearing the latest in resort jungle-safari wear, featuring tight-in-the-right-places-but-with-room-to-move black safari pants and a marvelous matching top with button-down pockets and mesh venting in the back, underarm, and cleavage areas. She had a brand-new two-idol-size fanny pack, wide-brim safari hat, and a designer backpack. She was as chic as someone heading out for a day in the wild could hope to be. At least Carol thought so.

Anyway, it wasn't so much the clothes, at least in this case, as it was the way you carried yourself. Carol held her head high, declined help in coming aboard, and promptly slipped on the front deck of the boat, falling on her ass.

* * *

There usually wasn't that much available in the way of rental boats in Key West. Sam had, of course, known some-one, and they were on their way toward the Ten Thousand

Islands in a roomy, shallow-draft center-console skiff with plenty of power.

Butch had done a lot of belly-aching about not wanting to go, but with Jose still on vacation up in Ratword, Sam didn't want to take anyone else from his bar staff. They were all reasonably competent, and he didn't want to lose them. So he told Butch to quit whining and be at the marina in the morning, or else hit the pavement.

Sam had gotten the guy he rented the boat from to help him the night before, loading tools he figured they might need. The weather was good, the boat was running fine, and they had plenty of gas. Sam wanted his treasure back.

* * *

Carol sat in the back behind the two men and tried to keep the wind from messing up her hair. The old man here had plenty of equipment along; maybe he actually knew what he was doing. She hoped so. She really wanted that third Chacmool.

Carol tried to think of all the things she was going to do with her new powers, but mostly just thought about different kinds of torture she would like to try out on Jeremy for leaving her alone with these two clowns. At first she wasn't so worried about old Sam having a stroke or something because Butch was along. But Macho Man here was acting like he was terrified of his own shadow since they'd left Key West. Not good.

* * *

Butch just about lost control of his bowels the first time a porpoise surfaced near the boat and that big dorsal fin came out of the water. He knew it was a porpoise, but it was still unnerving. Butch's normal method of dealing with his intense fear of sharks was to just never go near the water, which, when you live on an island, wasn't all that easy. Even when he worked at the jet-ski rental place, he wouldn't go out on the water; he just worked the ticket counter. Working at the Pink Snapper was about as far from sharks as you could get in Key West.

He saw porpoise fins several more times, and at least once he saw something that didn't look like a porpoise fin. He decided to just sit there in the seat next to Mr. Sam, look straight ahead, and keep a firm grip on the handholds while they were running. Butch tried to think about nice dark bar-rooms and asphalt parking lots. At least he was sure the old man and the cult bitch hadn't noticed how scared he was.

* * *

Sam wondered what was wrong with what's-his-name here. The boy was always so tough acting and ready to bust heads, but he was about to shit his drawers about some-thing out here. As long as he could dig when they got there.

He doubted the woman would be good for much except getting in the way. She had come through with the informa-tion on the house though; he had to give her that. Sam won-dered if she even knew that the house itself had been gone for years. He looked over at the big guy with the big nose sitting there with a white-knuckle death-grip on the boat and a strained look on his face, and made a mental note to find a new bouncer next week.

Chapter 51

Meanwhile, Back at the Motel

Jeremy had hidden under the bed when the phone first started ringing. He stayed there for a couple of hours after André had pounded on the door and told him he had an emergency phone call from a very angry woman. When he decided it was safe, he slipped out the back way of the motel and walked down the side streets to the Pink Snapper.

Chapter 52
Unhappy Campers

By mid-morning, when they got to the site of the old house, there was already a two-person kayak pulled up on the shore. Sam ran the skiff up on the beach about fifty feet further down and told the other two to wait in the boat.

A couple in their twenties, a skinny guy and a chubby girl, were standing a little ways from their campsite taking turns looking through binoculars at a pair of curlews in a tree across the channel. They had already broken camp, and their gear was all packed and sitting on the ground between them and where Sam had walked up.

"I'm sorry folks, there's no camping allowed here. I'm afraid you'll have to leave."

The young couple turned and stared at the old man in the big suit. The girl frowned.

"We checked with the Park Rangers three days ago before we came out here, and this is one of the places they said we could camp. Besides, you can see that other people have camped here."

She gave Sam a look like she wasn't about to be taking any shit off anyone not in a Park Ranger uniform.

God, but Sam hated dealing with the public. He had a lot to do and didn't need this.

"I'm sorry. I meant to say that smart-mouth little fat girls and their needle-dick boyfriends aren't allowed to camp here."

Sam pulled a Glock 9mm out of his shoulder holster and showed it to the couple whose mouths dropped open.

"Is that clear enough for you?"

Sam held the gun down and stepped to the side because the conversation seemed to be over. The two kayakers suddenly seemed anxious to comply with the new camping rules. They grabbed their stuff and made for the water. Sam looked around a bit at the old house site, and when he went back to the skiff, the kayak was gone.

* * *

"Can we get out now? I need to take a leak, and Ironman here looks like he wants to get out and kiss the ground."

Sam motioned them to come ashore.

"Judging by the way those people left I guess it would be safe to assume you didn't convince them to leave with your winning personality." Carol headed for the nearest bush.

Sam ignored her and told Butch to bring the metal detector and machetes first. Butch seemed to be happy to do anything that involved being on dry land again.

Chapter 53

A Cozy Cabin Waits for Mr. Small and Taco Bob

"Soup for what ails ya!"

When we got back to the cabin after our shark encounter, Mr. Small didn't have much to say; he just moved real slow, went inside, and sat there in his spot. He didn't seem to want me fussing around him, so since it was getting dark, I hurried over to the garden in the old man's dugout. When I got back I baited up a pole and managed to catch a little snapper before the bugs ate me up. I got a fire going in the stove and got us a pot of fish soup cooking.

The old man came over to the table and showed me in the light coming from the stove fire that he had stitched up his hand where he'd lost the finger. It looked like a good job, and the bleeding had almost stopped. He took some green paste from a bowl on the table and put it on the wound. I figured he must have made the paste while I was gone from one of the tuber things hanging from the ceiling.

Mr. Small didn't usually eat much anyhow, mostly fruit, so I wasn't surprised when he hardly touched the soup I set there for him. He went and sat in his spot and got real still like he was asleep.

I ate my fill and then lay there on the mat with just the little bit of light from the coals coming through the cracks in the stove. I listened to the skeeters buzzing outside the screens and thought about the fish I had caught that morning, the tarpon, the sharks, Mr. Small, and the rest of my life. I finally drifted off, and if I had any dreams, I didn't remember them in the morning.

* * *

Something had changed with that close call with the sharks, and it wasn't just that Mr. Small acted different. It felt like it was time for me to move on, but I stayed around with the old fella another day because I was worried about him. I kept asking him if he was going to be all right, but he just said that he was fine, just a little tired.

Mr. Small stayed outside most of the night again like he had when I first come around, and I wanted to take that as a sign he was feeling better. He did finally start acting a little more like his old self, and asked me the next day if I was going to share any of that whiskey I had before I left.

I couldn't help but look surprised, because I hadn't told the old man I had found a pint of liquor way up in the anchor locker when I had done my boat inventory. I figured the guy I bought the boat from must have stuck it in there and forgot about it. I hadn't said anything about leaving either.

The old man give me the first grin I had seen out of him in a while, and I knew he was going to be all right. It was okay for me to go.

Chapter 54

The House

The old Watson house was definitely gone all right. The whole place was mostly choked with Brazilian pepper, twelve feet tall in places, but they did manage to figure out where the house used to stand. Sam had Butch carry the metal detector and chop at the jungle in places, while he struggled through the underbrush and led the way. It was hot, dirty work. Carol found some shade by the boat and kept putting on more insect repellent while she earned her keep as lookout.

* * *

It was getting to be late afternoon, and in spite of the jungle, they had covered a good-sized portion of the area around where the house had stood. Sam was not a young man and was suffering from the heat. Butch was not an old man but was also suffering from the heat and getting real tired of carrying around the metal detector. He hoped they would find whatever it was they were looking for soon so they could get the hell out of there. He was also hoping they wouldn't find it, because then they would get back in the boat. He didn't even want to think about going all the way back to Key West, across all that water, in the dark.

* * *

Sam let his employee take a break for a sandwich and was using the detector himself around the cistern when he got something other than another beer can. He told the big lug to get his ass over there and do some digging. They had to cut some Brazilian pepper branches out of the way, and by the time the real digging was going on, Carol was there to whine about the bugs and heat again.

Sam was getting good at ignoring her and stayed on Butch's ass to keep digging. Butch didn't get down very far when he hit something hard and metal. Sam couldn't stand the suspense after all these years. He got down on his hands and knees, pulled several handfuls of dirt away, and uncovered a corner of the chest. He stood up and told Butch to dig. The woman came up closer.

"Shit! That's it, isn't it? Is that my idol?"

She grabbed Sam by the arm, and he pushed her away and drew his gun.

"Keep it up, and I'll give you a bug bite to remember!"

Butch saw the gun and dug harder. Carol stepped back and kept her mouth shut.

"That's enough! Now drag it out!"

Butch got a hold on the big rusty handle and strained hard getting the chest out of the hole.

"Use the shovel on it!"

A couple of hits with the shovel blade, and the lid came loose. Sam holstered his gun and pushed the sweaty young man to the side. He grabbed the lid and yanked it open.

* * *

Sand. Sam stuck his hands down in the sand inside the chest, and all he could feel in there was sand. He pushed it over and the sand spilled out on the ground. Sam ran his hands through the sand and spread it out on the ground. There was nothing in the chest except sand. Nothing.

* * *

Sam sat there for a while and stared at the empty chest. He mumbled something about how it was definitely his chest, and it was definitely empty. Then he stood up and looked in the hole for a while. He told them to gather up the tools, then started walking toward the boat like he was in a daze.

Carol decided not to say anything. She looked first in the chest, then the hole, making sure there weren't any Golden Chacmools in there that had been overlooked. There weren't.

Carol and Butch were heading back to the skiff when they heard gunshots up ahead. They dropped what they were carrying and ran toward the boat. Sam was there, pointing the gun at the water where the last couple of feet of a big gator were going under. The murky water was filled with bubbles and blood.

Carol stopped running when Sam turned around and faced her. He was still holding the gun.

"Jesus Christ, Sam! What the hell did you do that for?"

Sam looked pissed.

"Look, I've been having a real bad day, and I felt like shooting something. This just looked right, you okay with that?"

Carol turned around and went back to get what she'd been carrying. She swatted more mosquitoes and decided she wasn't having one of her better days either.

* * *

Butch followed Carol to get the stuff. It was going to be dark before they got back to Key West. It looked like nobody was having a good day.

Sam started the outboard after everything was loaded and slammed the motor in reverse to back away from the shore. Butch could still see some blood in the slow-moving water, and he had a flash of white-hot fear when he saw a big swirl, and a fin came out of the water just downstream from the boat. He really hoped it was a porpoise.

* * *

The bow of the skiff came loose from the shore and the boat moved backward a few feet. The outboard jumped, made a bad noise, and stalled. Sam swore and ran the tilt up on the motor so he could see what was going on. He stepped to the back of the boat and saw a big log just under the water moving with the current and a very bent propeller on the outboard. There was no way they were going any- where like that. Sam grabbed a hammer out of the toolbag, and motioned to his barroom bully.

"Take this and lean out over the back of the boat and try to bang that propeller back in line."

The big guy just sat there and clutched the seat with both hands with a horrified look on his face. He stared at

Sam and slowly shook his head. It obviously was going to take more that a gun to get him to lean out over the edge of the boat. Carol had moved to the front and seemed to be trying to look inconspicuous.

"I've got to do everything around here, don't I?" Sam grabbed the outboard with one hand and leaned way out over the stern but couldn't get a good angle with the hammer. He looked back at what's-his-name sitting there with a death-grip on his seat.

"Brian, pull yourself together! Come over here and grab hold of my belt and —" Sam's hand slipped on the outboard's cowling and he was in the water. The boat had drifted out, away from the shore, and was slowly moving along with the current. Sam hadn't done any swimming in years, but it came right back and he splashed his way over to the boat. At least from the water, he had the right angle and started banging on the propeller with the hammer.

"Goddamn it, Butch, I told you to —"

Suddenly, Sam was gone. He just disappeared under the water. Carol was on her feet and headed for the back of the boat. About ten feet away, a foot came out of the dark water, then a big fin, then a hand. There was a lot of blood in the water. The water boiled with shark fins and shark tails, and then it was over.

Carol stood on the back seat of the boat with her hands on her hips.

"Well, that sucks! He did say he was having a bad day. I guess he was right!"

Butch started to cry. Carol came over and patted him on the shoulder.

"Don't be sad, at least he got your name right finally. What the hell's wrong with you anyway? Haven't you ever seen anyone eaten by sharks before? Didn't you ever see the movie Jaws?"

Butch lay down on the floor of the boat and went into the fetal position, sobbing uncontrollably. Carol stood there looking down at him.

"Hmm, guess not. Oh well."

She got her cellphone out of her backpack and punched the number for the Monroe County Sheriff's Department, which she'd thought to write down on the cellphone cover. She hadn't thought to check her calling plan range, however, and while Butch sobbed and the boat drifted, she ran the battery down trying in vain to get something besides a dial tone.

*   *   *

It was a hellish night on the boat. The mosquitoes were out in full force as soon as it started getting dark. The bites were bad, but the incessant buzzing was maddening. Then, if things weren't bad enough, a thunderstorm blew in and they got soaked from the rain.

Butch refused to acknowledge Carol and spent the night lying on the floor of the boat, curled up in his own night-mares, sobbing and moaning. The boat was drifting out the river slowly, and Carol tried to cover her head with a towel as she lay on the front deck. The hard fiberglass was uncom-fortable enough, and the bugs made sleep almost impossi-ble. Sometime during the night Carol took the fanny pack off and did a little whimpering of her own before falling into a fitful sleep.

Chapter 55

More Good-byes for Taco Bob

"I'm sure gonna miss the ol' fella!"

Mr. Small and me sat up late that last night, sipping whiskey, talking by the light of the stove there in the cabin, listening to the thunder from a storm off in the distance, and me trying to do a better job of listening overall. He showed me his left hand where he'd lost the little finger, and it looked like it was going to heal as well as could be expected.

Earlier he'd given me an old cloth bag with some of his vegetables and a few of the little dried root things in it to take with me. I tried to give him my toolbox and tools, but he said he didn't really need anything, and anyway, he already had something I'd given him and held up the little pliers tool.

There was a small tarnished statue the old man used as a doorstop. He went over, picked it up, and stuck it in the vegetable sack.

"I'm all out of souvenir T-shirts, but you can take this to remember your visit to the Ten Thousand Islands and the Everglades."

I'd been meaning to ask him about that weird little metal statue that looked kind of like an animal with a person's head. I didn't think the timing was right at the moment, and anyway, I was getting a little choked up about leaving.

"It's just some old thing I found a long time ago. Maybe it'll bring you some luck."

He took the bag out to my boat and set it down on the floor so I wouldn't forget it in the morning, in case I left before he came in.

We sat by the stove and finished the little bottle of whiskey as the last of the thunder boomed off in the distance. He told me if I was passing that way again to be sure to stop by, and worked up a little grin over that. I told him I would, and then he give me real careful instructions how to find my way back out to the coast.

Mr. Small got to his feet, and I stood up too. He stuck out his hand and we shook and gave a good hug, then he was out the door.

My eyes were tired, and I knew how good I was going to sleep on that mat. I lay down and was sound asleep before I even got my shoes off.

Chapter 56

In the Night

Without a sound, the small vessel moved up alongside the boat drifting down the slow wide river. It was a dark, cloudy night. Other than the ever-present hum of the insects, the only sounds were the waves lapping against the boat and the occasional moans from the people lying inside.

A small dark head with calm steady eyes came up over the side of the boat, then a hand reached down and slowly lifted out a small bag with straps on each end.

* * *

Later, the same hand carefully reached inside another boat. The hand touched the one solid heavy object in the old cloth bag and slowly, silently, took it from the bag and over the side into the darkness.

The small dugout canoe slipped through the mangrove swamp like a shadow. Its lone diminutive occupant standing in the rear, poling steadily and seemingly without effort.

There was a platform in the mangroves, only a few feet above the water. There was another canoe there as well. On the platform was an old man sleeping, lying on his back. The little person was just barely tall enough to see the old man from where he stood in his canoe. Steady, silent hands took the heavy little figures from the bag and placed one by each of the old man's ears. Then both hands gently set the third figure over the eyes.

* * *

Just before first light, one of the figures went back in the bag of vegetables, and the little bag with the other two went just underneath.

Chapter 57

Still More Leaving for Taco Bob

"It was time for me to go."

In the morning I got in my boat and started poling my way on back out to civilization. I had waited around to see if Mr. Small was going to come back to the house, but I got a real strong feeling he wasn't.

I didn't know if I had enough gas to make it back to Key West, so I did like the old man had told me the night before and ran north along the coast to Chokoloskee to get gas. I was running along the coast, enjoying the feeling of the wind in my face on a beautiful day. I was thinking that according to my chart, I was close to the place I had been looking for at one time, where the old house used to be. I was looking over that way and saw what looked like someone in a boat on the edge of the mangroves, standing up, waving. If I hadn't been looking that way, I'd have never even seen 'em.

When I got closer I could see it was a boat drifting there with a young couple who looked a bit rough. They were both skeeter-bit real bad. I figured they must have spent the night out there and got that thunderstorm that had come through.

Their boat had a bad prop, and I told them I'd try to fix it, but they didn't want any of that. They wanted me to pull their boat back in.

The fella was a big guy, and he sure didn't look like he was enjoying himself at all. He didn't say much; he just sat there in the bottom of the boat and looked real unhappy.

The woman said she wanted to ride with me and climbed aboard. We tied-off their boat to mine and started in. She sat right down on my bag of vegetables on the floor behind me. I felt so sorry for them bedraggled-looking folks, I didn't have the heart to tell her not to sit there.

I finished the run to Chok and let those folks off at a public dock next to a little store. The woman said thanks and headed off to use the phone, still looking a little shaky. The guy just got out of the boat and went and sat on the ground.

Chapter 58

Back

It had been the worst night of her life. When she realized it was morning, Carol checked on her Chacmools and they were gone. She freaked, and completely lost it, tearing the boat apart looking for them. Butch was a total loss. The big tough-guy had been so paralyzed with fear all night that he'd wet his pants lying there on the floor of the boat.

After breaking down and crying until she got sick, Carol was looking over the far edge of sanity when she heard the fisherman's boat and started waving a towel.

* * *

There was something hard under the cloth bag that Carol was sitting on in the bottom of the stranger's boat. She reached her hand underneath and pulled out her fannypack with both Chacmools inside.

There was still something in the bag digging into her ass, but Carol was so shocked to find her Chacmools again that she didn't even care. She looked at the fisherman standing in front of her running the boat and started to ask him if he knew how her pack got in his boat, but she was feeling a little dizzy and wasn't really sure of anything at that point.

* * *

When Carol got to Chokoloskee, she immediately called and put a stop on Jeremy's credit card. She got a ride to Tampa, and the next day she was back in LA. She was still feeling half-sick from her night on the boat and thought she might have a fever.

Carol had always bruised easily, and she'd checked the whopper she found on her ass in the airport bathroom. Back in her room at the Spider Cult mansion, she backed up to a mirror for a better look. Whatever had been in that bag sure had left an odd bruise.

Carol got one of the Chacmools out of its hiding place, looked in the mirror, and put the Chacmool on the bruise. It was a perfect match.

Chapter 59

Even More Leaving and Good-byes for Taco Bob

"I swear I seen that kid somewhere before!"

I got my gas at the little marina in Chok after I made sure the folks I had brought in were going to be all right. There was a little kid hanging around, kind of an Indian-looking kid with real shiny eyes. He slipped up real quiet; I hadn't noticed he was there until I looked up. He didn't have much to say, just mostly hung back where I couldn't get a real good look at him. When I got ready to leave I waved good-bye, and he lit up a big smile and started waving back. I got the boat turned around and looked back to give him another wave, since he seemed to like that so much. I seen he had a little friend standing there, about the same size. When I waved they both lit up big grins and the new kid, he give me a wink and started waving too. I was moving out the channel by then, but I was still close enough to plainly see the second kid was missing the little finger on his left hand.

Chapter 60
Key West as Home for Taco Bob
"Home is where the truck is!"

I made that long run back down the coast of the Ten Thousand Islands and across Florida Bay toward Key West. The weather couldn't have been nicer for a boat ride, hardly a cloud in the sky and calm seas all the way back. I had plenty to think about with all the things I'd done and seen the last few days, not to mention what might be waiting for me back in the Conch Republic. But the thing that stuck in my mind most was how I'd finally looked at my hands in a dream my last night in the little cabin and had my first real lucid dream. I was ready to agree with the folks that said it felt just as real as everyday. I could feel a new confidence coming on, like the way you feel after finally doing something you been after for a long time.

The sun had just about given it up for another day by the time I got both feet on dry land again. I was bone tired from the long boat ride and decided to splurge and get myself a motel room for the night. I took a cab over to one that looked like it ought to have a vacancy, but there was a little bald guy in there having a bad argument with the fella behind the counter about his credit card or something.

So I decided to go on over to Pete's sister's place and check on my old truck. She was home by herself, with her husband and kid off to the ball field, and insisted I come inside and have something to eat. While she warmed up some leftovers I got cleaned up and settled in at the dining room table.

"The police caught the guys that'd been breaking into houses while you were gone. Just this morning, in fact."

"Well, that's good news. I was pretty sure it wasn't me doing it."

I hadn't realized how hungry I was, and started in doing some serious damage to the plate full of jerk chicken, scalloped potatoes, and corn on the cob. She gave me a look and sat down at the table.

"Caught the two guys breaking into the Hemingway House. Told the police they were just early for the tour, but the surveillance camera had them hauling off books. Turns out they'd been breaking into writer's houses to steal first edition books to sell on those online auctions."

This was sounding familiar.

"Was there one guy real big and the other small with shifty eyes?"

She nodded, and I thought she was going to ask how I knew, but she went on with more news instead.

"Pete's been asking about you. Says he's doing real fine up there in North Carolina, and you should go on up there sometime and do a little fishing with him."

This was sounding good. She walked out of the room to get me another glass of iced tea and called out from the kitchen.

"That oriental man, Hop, called again too. Said you should get in touch next time you passed through here, let him know how you're getting along."

I was just finishing up when she came back in and set the glass of tea and a big slice of key lime pie in front of me.

"Been some woman calling here while you been gone too. Said her name was Mary Ann. She says to tell you she'd really like to hear from you." She gave me a questioning look, and I came up with a little smile and a shrug.

I tore into that pie and thanked her for one of the better meals I'd come across in a while. She got me up to speed on a little of the latest goings-on around town: One of the Marty Manatee impersonators was running for mayor, there was a For Sale sign in front of the old hotel everyone said was haunted, and some of the wild chickens around town had taken to roosting on the Southernmost Marker and were making the national news. I didn't even realize it at first, but I was paying real close attention to everything she said.

After I finished eating, I gave her a couple handfuls of homegrown vegetables out of the bag that Mr. Small had given me. She looked at those kind of gnarly-looking carrots and stuff and smiled funny. I pulled the little doorstop figurine out of the bag and showed her that. She looked at it real close and said it might be gold, and it might be worth some money. I told her it had sentimental value to me and I doubted I'd likely be giving it up anytime soon. She held it up to the light and I thought of something. When she handed it back I finally realized what it was about the shape. There was no doubt about it, the head looked like a woman, but the body looked to me just like a possum with the tail curled up underneath.

Pete's sister gave me a paper she'd written my messages and some phone numbers down on, and a few pieces of mail that had found me somehow. She offered to clean up my little gold souvenir from the swamp with some metal polish, so I handed it over. I thanked her some more, then headed out to my truck parked there in the side yard.

I got about halfway across the driveway when I heard a metallic click off to the side, kind of like the sound you'd expect the trigger cover of a missile to make as it hit pavement. I stopped in my tracks and slowly turned.

It was getting dark, but I could plainly see Lenny crouched down there on the driveway holding up one of those TOW missile launchers on his shoulder. Of course, George stood there next to him, sighting the thing my way, with one hand on what must have been the trigger and grinning to beat the band.

"Evening, Taco Bob!"

"Evening, George, Lenny. I thought you fellas were caught, and in the slammer."

George looked up, but kept his hand on the trigger.

"You know what they say about it being hard to keep a good criminal down. We were only in there a few hours. It was laundry day at the jail, so we kinda slipped out in a laundry cart."

I noticed a laundry van parked next door.

"Hid out for a while over in a warehouse on the Navy base, found this little beauty still in the crate. If you wouldn't mind holding still for another minute and putting your hands up, I'm just about done reading the instructions here."

From twenty feet away, I doubted even George could miss. I looked behind me at the vacant lot across the street and miles of open ocean after that.

"You seem to have this thought out some, George. I'm impressed." I could see George's lips moving as he read. "Lady inside the house here lays out a mean spread. Jerk chicken, scalloped potatoes, pie —"

Lenny and the missile started shaking a little. George dropped the instruction book and clamped his hands over his partner's ears.

"Don't listen to him none, Lenny!" He gave me his meanest look. "Don't be starting none of that stuff now, Taco! We got ya fair and square this time!"

I was thinking about making a break for it as George sighted in on my chest again. Only problem was going to be trying to outrun a missile.

"Say your prayers, Taco Bob, this is the end!"

I noticed a light back over the trees, then a noise. Suddenly there was a spotlight glaring down from a helicopter and wind whipping around. One of the rare times I was glad to see the police. They hovered overhead in that noisy machine and yelled stuff on a loudspeaker about not moving and getting on the ground.

Poor George couldn't believe it, standing there looking up with his mouth hanging open. He grabbed the back of the launcher and pointed that awesome looking missile up at the chopper, which took a hard left and was gone. He redirected his cold stare and missile back at me, but in all the noise and confusion, the yard had filled up with armed and excitable police.

George looked around at all them guns pointed at him, and at me still standing there with my hands up. He smiled big at the cops and started raising his hands.

"Looks like you got us, boys!"

Which made everybody but me and George relax just a bit. George came up with a blood-curdling yell and made a grab at the launcher just as I hit the deck. I could feel the heat from the missile on my back as it roared by. George and Lenny were occupied with a lot of police doing a pile-up on them and the empty launcher, but I sat up in time to see the explosion out over the water.

They arrested the Daltons, and me for good measure, and we all went down to the police station for a few rounds of question and answer in the interrogation room. Finally, well after midnight, they decided to believe what Pete's sister had told them over the phone and cut me loose.

It was turning into another long day for me. I started walking the three miles back to my truck hoping to hitch a ride. I got about halfway back when an old station wagon stopped.

"I'm trying to get over to the other side of the island, over by Mango Street."

"Get in, I know where that is."

Big fella driving looked somehow familiar wearing a shower cap and what looked to be a kilt.

"Thanks, much obliged."

"Don't mention it. I'm scouting around looking for a place to open a restaurant."

My weary mind figured it odd to be looking for real estate in the dark, though it was cooler with less traffic. But I didn't mention any of that, I was just glad to have a ride with someone who drove slow and never seemed to take his eyes off the road.

When we got to Pete's sister's place I thanked the man and made my way through all the crime scene tape over to my truck. I climbed into the little camper on the back and there was my little gold doorstop sitting on the bed. I put it under my pillow and stretched out big thinking about where I've been and what I had going next.

I drifted off to sleep in a little while, looking forward to the next day, and the rest of my life.

For information on books by Robert Tacoma:
www.tacobob.com

Acknowledgments

A tip of the hat to the folks who helped in the long, arduous journey that is this book. AG for the kind words and advice early on. Bart for loaning me one of the all-time worst books ever written. Annie for her relentless criticism and pickiness. Sandra for noticing things above and beyond normal human comprehension. And last, but not least, SLM for everything.

Robert Tacoma has been working and playing in Florida all his adult life, and he isn't done yet. The book you hold in your hands is the result of his life experiences and rampant imagination. He lives in central Florida, and all his pets have run away.